Indecent
Deception

JUDITH PRICE

JUDITH PRICE

To all the innocent, may you find solace, hope and peace

PROLOGUE

"If you control the oil, you can control entire nations or groups of nations." —Henry K.

Istanbul, Turkey, Two Weeks Earlier

Pain spiked through her each time her bare foot smacked the grunge that smeared along the alleyway. She couldn't stop—she had no choice. Run. An entanglement of wire hummed, buzzing as she ran through the obstacle course of strewn garbage. Tiny sparks burst above her as the rain tapped on the live wires. They were chasing her, that much she knew. The run-down shanties checkered the dark alleyway. Rain pelted onto the tin roofs that held the thin walls in place. She could see the street ahead. She had to move fast. Shuffled garbage flew behind her as she ran. The alley groaned from the wind. She didn't look back; she had to keep her focus, she had to move, she had to survive.

A man coughed as she leaped over the wet, pajama-like clothes that clung to his legs. A lone shopkeeper stopped rolling up a steel barrier door and stared as she ran past him. She was naked. Small spikes of pain ripped through the balls of her feet, but she didn't care—she'd felt worse pain. She hooked to the right, back into the next alley, and zigzagged to her left around an old wooden cart covered in plastic. She knew she must be close to her embassy. She had visualized the directions he had told her. Her lungs burned with adrenaline as they expanded against her bruised ribs. It had to be close, and she knew how to run—knew how to calculate. They'd let her in if she could get to the American Embassy. She'd be safe. At least, she hoped she would.

She rounded the corner and abruptly stopped on the street. Her arms flailed backward, trying to balance herself. Brushing the dirty, wet strands of hair from her eyes, she blinked out the raindrops and leaned forward, looking cautiously around and down the road. Confusion clouded her thoughts; something didn't feel right. Her breath fogged the cool air. She could see the concrete guardhouse inside a tall black steel fence surrounding the embassy grounds in the distance. Diagonal yellow stripes on the concrete-bordered base outlined the massive hill the American Embassy was perched on, some hundred feet above. Giant spotlights lit up the sides of the gigantic fort-like structure.

She looked around; the street was empty. Rows of shops sagged from age as the dark of night chilled the air. She huffed, sucked in another chestful of air, then hobbled over the gravel road. Adrenaline masked the pain of the sharp stones jammed between her raw toes. She started to move fast toward the building; her wet hair slapped her shoulders, and for the first time since she was taken, hope began to surge through her.

And just when hope began to warm her soul, reaching down into the depths of it, bright lights blinked on, blinding her. An engine roared before a black van screeched to a stop, turning sideways two feet before her. The van door was wide open, and two men jumped out. One man grabbed her hair, pulling her off her feet backward. Her skin ripped as her body skidded on the wet stone.

"No. No. No!" she screamed as the other man grabbed her legs. She struggled to pull her arms and legs as if entangled in a spider's web at the mouth of hell. She struggled and grunted and screamed. "Leave me alone—"

A fist slammed into her face. Pain burst across her temple, and tiny stars flashed before her eyes. Blackness. They threw her into the van. The door scraped metal on metal as it slid shut.

CHAPTER ONE

Simple-minded are the people who believe that what they see transpiring in the mask of life is a reality. This belief is a betrayal to themselves. Why do they not question coincidences or what is not plausible? Why then do we accept the evil and greed of humankind over societies, over morals, and over our true selves?

Tucson, Arizona, United States

Jill Oliver's hands shook as she fumbled with her key. The folder of Europol documents balanced under one arm slipped half an inch, then spilled its contents over the sunbaked Arizona sidewalk.

"Damn it!" Jill crouched down to sweep up the papers. She didn't have time for this. Her flight to Istanbul left in an hour.

She took a deep breath to steady her jangled nerves, then shoved the last of the documents into the folder and the folder into her bag. The Uber driver waiting curbside honked his horn and pointed to his watch.

"I'm coming!" Jill shouted. Under her breath, she added, "Thanks for the help, buddy." She dragged her suitcase along the sidewalk toward the popped trunk of the car.

"Jill Oliver!"

Jill spun at the intruding voice and dropped into a fighting stance. Instinct. She couldn't help it—too many years of Muay Thai training.

The stranger who'd yelled her name skidded to a halt, then stepped back with his palms held up, fingers spread wide. "Whoa, sorry. Just trying to catch you before you got in the car."

Jill didn't relax her posture. "Who are you? What do you want?"

The stranger held his hand for a shake but didn't take another step toward Jill. She eyed him. "Alfred Maxter, author."

"I'm late for my flight." She frowned at his outstretched hand but didn't take it. But she did ease up on her posture. "What do you want?"

Maxter choked out a laugh. "Yes, yes." His hand dropped back to his side. "Straight to the point. I like that."

Somehow, Jill doubted it.

Maxter continued. "Well...I guess I'll jump right to the point, then. I'm the official biographer for Matthew McGregor, and I need to speak to you."

Jill's gut lurched. Her hands began to tremble as her stomach tapped its way up her esophagus. "Matthew McGregor?"

"Yes, you know he's in—"

"Prison. Of course, I know." She shot Maxter a death glare. Did he honestly think it was possible she could have forgotten the psychopath who'd tried to murder her?

Tried and almost succeeded.

Maxter chuckled again, and Jill saw beads of sweat forming along his brow. "Yes, of course. My apologies. It's just... well, Matthew would like to speak to you."

"Speak to me?" Jill's stomach began to kick the back of her throat.

Swallow. Deep breaths. She forced herself to practice her yoga breathing. Slow your heart rate, Jill. Don't let Matthew have control—have control again.

"Ah yeah." Maxter licked his lips. "He insists I bring you to the prison to see him." He choked out another laugh, and the sweat trickled down his temples. "Quite persistent, Matthew is. I'm sure you understand."

Oh, she understood, alright.

"Matthew, huh?" Jill recovered enough to pick up her suitcase and shove it into the car's trunk. "On a first-name basis with the psycho killer, are we?"

"I..." Maxter stared blankly. "I'm his biographer."

"Lucky you." Jill pushed past him and opened the back door of the car.

"Ms. Oliver, wait!" Maxter said, moving toward her. "Matthew—Mr. McGregor—is determined to see you. Insistent. Perhaps we could make arrangements so you'd be comfortable meeting with him."

"There aren't enough arrangements on the planet, buddy." Jill twisted to step into the car.

"Wait!" Maxter pushed himself in her path, making Jill stand upright. His face was inches in front of hers. She could smell his desperation. "He's refusing to speak to me further about the book until I get you to the prison. You must come with me." He took a handkerchief from his pocket and mopped his glistening forehead. "Please. Perhaps if your husband accompanied you to the prison? You'd feel safe."

Jill's heart kicked. David. She closed her eyes for a second. She imagined feeling safe in David's arms the way she used to—safe from McGregor, safe from PTSD, safe from the evil doings of the terrorists she profiled in her job.

"Ms. Oliver?"

Jill opened her eyes again. She felt her expression harden to steel. "My husband is dead, Mr. Maxter. If you were a professional, you would already know this. It's been all over the news, and I'm late for my flight. Now get the hell out of my way."

CHAPTER TWO

Tucson, Arizona, United States

David Brown scanned the room, looking for surveillance equipment. Doing this was more out of habit than anything else, really. He knew this room was secure. It's where they met—where they always met when something was not going quite right. The room was in a classified building, in a classified location, in a classified area in Tucson, Arizona.

"She was getting too close, Paul," David said and leaned in. "I had no choice." He slapped his hands on his dark green army fatigues. "Jill was too close, and Stan was getting suspicious. I had to disappear."

"We always have a choice, David." Paul Grant didn't even look up from his desk. He continued to leaf through the files on it. "Sometimes we make the choices that are best for our country, and sometimes"—he dropped one folder onto the top of the stack and leveled his gaze at David—"we do what's best for ourselves."

David leaned back and studied Paul. "Someone must have been giving her information because how the hell did she know where to find me—find us?"

Paul's brow furrowed. "How long have we worked together now... two years, give or take?"

David nodded. "You know I didn't come up with this gig. You came looking for me. I can't believe I've waited so long for payback. Hard to believe you let me off my leash only three months ago." David held Paul's poker-faced stare.

Paul crossed his legs and looked directly at David. "I wonder if Stan knew. It was almost too much of a coincidence for him, don't you think... you running into your father while on assignment for Time, in Afghanistan of all places?" Paul's lip curled to the right. "I guess you must have pulled off an Academy Award-winning performance to evade his suspicion. What was the name of the article again?" Paul chuckled. "You know, the one you told Stan you were working on to run into him conveniently?"

David thought about it. He was great at telling stories. It's how he survived his father's wrath throughout his childhood. Maybe it's why he became a journalist. He did not know. And no one cared anyway. Certainly not his family and the government, but his new unofficial employer. "A Soldier's Life, After Afghanistan and the Family Impact." David tilted his head and shrugged.Paul smiled. "You know we work well as a team. You are one of my best in the field," Paul said unconvincingly. "You did well, given the circumstances. He trusted you, David."

David looked down at the floor and thought about his father. He wondered if he really did gain Stan's trust, and for a fleeting second, David's heart kicked. He snapped back up. "I don't know, Paul. I thought I had him pegged. But... my mission is over now, isn't it? You've read my report." David crossed his arms and contemplated again. It wasn't the first time he wished he hadn't chosen to work for his government.

"Well, yes, but there is a little bit of a problem."

David sighed. He knew. Jill.

He hadn't known she was physically looking for him until she showed up in Afghanistan with Zayed. Zayed Mohammed, or so they called him, was one of them. Officially an intelligence broker, a peddler of intel, or so David was told. He didn't know what to believe right now, but he sure as hell would find out. It wasn't about himself, really, or maybe it was. The shrinks would have to figure it all out after he was done—after he finished the mission—his mission. And who knew, maybe when he got to the truth—discovered what the truth really was—well, he didn't want to think about that right now.

"Your wife, David. Jill." Paul glanced at the files on the table and then back to David.

"I know; she got in the way. But you have to admit, she pretty much ended my mission. God knows how she did that. Someone must have been giving her intel." David thought of Zayed again.

Paul's look was questioning, and he paused before he said, "You don't know?"

"Know what?"

Paul's eyes narrowed. "You knew your wife had worked for the FBI before she became a US Marshal, right?"

"Yeah, she was an intelligence analyst or something like that, a desk jockey."

Paul leaned back and folded his arms, then tilted his head inquisitively. "Did you know she was a Remote Viewer?" Silence. "Geez, David, she's your wife, for Christ's sake. You're married to her and don't know what she did for the FBI?"

David scowled; he knew goddamn well why he'd married her and huffed out, "A Remote Viewer?"

Paul's chair creaked as he leaned back again. A minute had passed, and no one spoke. Paul leaned forward, grabbed a file from the stack on his desk, and tossed it to David. "Here. Read this. It's about your wife. Flip to the second-to-last page." David was shuffling the pages as Paul continued. "The Remote Viewing Department, back then, was a fairly new division at the FBI, set up to assist the then-Homeland Security." Paul leaned back in his chair and shook his head. "I can't believe you didn't know."

David thumbed to the page and began to read. After a few minutes, he slammed the file shut. "A psychic? A goddamn psychic? You've got to be kidding me. What, she followed a crystal ball halfway around the world?"

"Not a psychic, David. A Remote Viewer. In fact, her job title was indeed Crime Analyst. But you do know that we humans have a natural psychic ability. I don't, but it appears your wife was a natural. She and her team got results for the bureau. Of course, only some of the results are in this file. Some are still classified."

David felt an are-you-kidding-me look grow on his face.

Paul continued. "And by all accounts, your wife excels with her ability. It's how she allegedly followed you. Look..." Paul pushed the folder back towards David. "Read it, page five." David flipped open the file to the page as Paul continued. "She had met with a CIA case officer in Dubai, Frank Wells. I met Frank back in the early days of our careers. He's a straight shooter. I guess her old boss, Eric Wallace at the FBI, reported her attempts to find you to Frank. And based on this brief, it appears she used her skills quite well."

David pulled the second report stapled in the file's top corner and flipped through the pages. David's eyes skimmed. "Kushka," he hushed. "Yeah, Zayed was helping her. Bastard. That explains how she knew where I was."

"Read on," Paul said.

David continued reviewing the docket and spoke as he read. "The report says a lot of things. Things are missing. It's not an accurate account of what I was doing or, frankly, where I was. How could she just dream up where I was? It's bullshit, Paul." David threw the brief back onto the table and leaned back, resting his elbows on the armrests. He silently tapped his fingertips together in a robotic beat and watched Paul.

"I know this was a hard assignment to complete, given the target. I mean, well, you were about to discover the funding arm behind Stan's operation if your wife... ah, Jill, hadn't gotten involved. All we have right now is Stan Brown. He's being treated very well in Guantanamo." Paul smirked. "But so far, nothing. He keeps whining like a stuck pig, repeating to himself that he was just the mule." Paul paused and stared at David. David crossed his arms and listened. "There is nothing we can do about that for the time being. But we have assets at 'the Bay.' He'll crack soon." Paul shifted and said nothing.

David mimicked him and shifted. He wasn't about to say anything; he knew the truth about 'the Bay.' Other than this new information about Jill, he'd heard it all before. He knew what was going on. Damn right, he knew.

Paul continued. "Right now, our concern is that we think Stan's group is aware of Jill's involvement and that perhaps she was given intel that led to Stan Brown's capture. She's been interviewed extensively, and she swears she has nothing. No information that they may want. All we know at this point is that a plan to execute a nuclear device was in play, and the rogue Chechen mercenaries would make it look like the Russians had set it off. That plan, you know, was thwarted with the capture of Stan Brown. But we know these mercenaries followed you and Jill before the apprehension. The chatter is giving us little right now, but from what we see, we need to get you out of here immediately. They'll be looking for both of you. You both might be in danger.

"Both of us?" David sat up stiffly. "In danger? What makes you think that? How do they know where I am? Why would they even care about Jill?" He grunted.

Paul glanced down at the files and then back at David. A serious look clouded his face. David caught it and slightly stiffened. "It's why we brought you back to Tucson, David." Paul leaned forward, picked another file off the table, and handed it to him. "We want you to recruit Jill, David. You knew this was coming." David opened the folder. "The first page in the folder is your next assignment, and your target is Jill Oliver. It's not a coincidence that Jill's next assignment is in Turkey. You know that's where you were heading before we called you in."

David looked at Paul squarely as he watched him reach into his top pocket, pull out a folded Post-it note, and hand it to him. "You'd better hurry. She leaves in less than two hours."

CHAPTER THREE

Tucson International Airport

Jill scanned her assignment documents in the Europol folder as the Uber driver negotiated the airport traffic. It was simple stuff: logistics. Nothing about her assignment. This troubled Jill, and she frowned. Were they taking it easy on her? Did they think she was fragile, or did they not trust her yet? Then an even more unsettling thought wormed its way into her consciousness. Was she fragile?

She snapped the folder closed and stuffed it back into her bag. No one would have described Jill Oliver as fragile three years ago. Not when she'd been a kick-ass Remote Viewer for the FBI, part of the RV program's pilot team, tackling the most challenging cases and putting her Navajo gifts to good use.

But now? After everything that happened with McGregor and then losing David, the Remote Viewing image of the fireball in the desert, which had consumed Zayed, flared back to her awareness. She shuddered and tried to force it away.

"Ma'am?" the Uber driver cut into Jill's thoughts with broken English. "Tucson International Airport, ma'am." He stopped the car at the international departures curb.

Jill took a deep breath. "Right." She lugged her physical and emotional baggage onto the sidewalk, swiped her phone, and tapped. "Thanks. I've given you a tip."

He nodded, glanced down at his phone, then pulled away.

Jill looked back at her phone to check the time. Damn it. She hoped they'd hold the flight for her. Surely they would for a Europol agent. Security should be easy, at least.

Suddenly, she felt it. She'd felt it during these past few weeks. Someone was watching her.

Jill did her surveillance scans. She started her round-the-clock scans. Three o'clock. There, she almost missed him; he was so well hidden in the shadows. But there he was, and she could feel his gaze on her. This guy knew what he was doing, the way he used the angle of the setting sun to find the deepest shadow in which to disappear—the darkest corner from which to watch her.

The irrational fear that Matthew McGregor was somehow the man standing in that black enclave rose inside Jill's mind.

No. It's not him. He's in prison.

That jerk Maxter had confirmed it not fifteen minutes before. Jill couldn't allow the anxiety to overwhelm her. Not again.

But then, who the hell was this guy watching her now, and why?

The man took a step into the dusky sunlight and then another. Another step, and his face was fully visible. Familiar. Unexpected. Impossible. Jill's mouth dropped open, and her phone slipped from her fingers. The glass screen cracked on the sidewalk.

The man was David.

CHAPTER FOUR

NATO, Outside of Brussels, Belgium

The large, bright orange square building sat on a four-corner intersection. Besides the bright color, it looked like any ordinary structure in the quaint city. Small windows checkered all sides of the building. Inside the front foyer, the security desk seemed too small for the vast, open room. A lone security guard spoke Flemish as he buzzed the tall man through the large bulletproof door. It thudded shut as the man entered the long corridor and the first room on the right.

"What do we know so far?" the man sitting at a metal table asked as the tall man entered.

"We have what we need in place, sir," he said, handing the folder to the Commander of the Commander-in-Chief.

"And the shipment? It may be our last one for a while."

"It's ready."

"Everything? You know this is not just an ordinary shipment."

The tall man nodded.

The Commander opened the folder and then arched an eyebrow while reading. "The CIA... hmmm... Don't worry about the CIA. They won't get in our way."

The man read in silence and then said, "David Brown. Isn't he one of ours?"

"Well, he does bat with the Yankees, sir."

The Commander leaned back in his chair. "If he doesn't want to play, you know what to do. We've been implementing this plan for months and can't rely on non players. What do we know about him?"

The tall man sat down and nodded toward the folder. "He is currently classified as AWOL, and we are trying to apprehend him to determine if our counterintelligence is correct. He could be in deep cover; he's that sort of operative."

"I thought this was all taken care of?" the Commander snarled. A beat, and then, "Well, is it or not?"

"Everything is under control, sir, and we have the chatter. We're zeroing in on him."

"Chatter! You know we can't rely on chatter. Someone must know where he is." The Commander glanced back down at the page in the folder. He closed the folder and handed it back to the tall man. "Find him and find him now. This must be taken care of before the shipment leaves," he demanded. "Hire whoever you need to, and if you can't find him, find his wife, Jill Oliver."

CHAPTER FIVE

Tucson International Airport

The air was stifling on the still-hot August night. The cacophony of airport sounds echoed, bouncing off the yellow bricks of the exterior walls.

Jill shrieked as David pulled her into the shadows. She twisted, jerking her arms out of his grasp. Jill's training instinct made her pull the first punch. The sound of Jill's fist connecting with David's chin reverberated. "Ouch. Dammit!" She shook her hand in pain. She twisted around, held her fighting stance, and faced him.

David grabbed his jaw and winced. "I guess I deserved that."

Jill took two steps back, looked at him, and squared herself again. But David looked far from menacing, rubbing his jaw with a half-cocked smile. She looked at him; malice moved through her, then began draining onto the dirt. "You're alive?" Her voice sharpened.

He moved slowly toward her. "Yes, Jill, I'm alive," he said, almost purring. "I ah... I wanted to tell you sooner. But it wasn't safe. It's still not safe."

Jill took a step backward. "But... but—"

"I can explain, Jill; it's not how it seems, but we don't have much time. We need to act now." He reached toward her, resting his hands on her shoulders, and looked at her squarely. "You know I work for the CIA and was briefed on that. And, for the record, I want you to know... I'm not working with my father."

Jill wanted to pull away, but before she could think, before she could feel, he wrapped his arms around her. His warmth pulsed hot blood through her veins, and Jill began to sob for the first time in the past weeks. David released his embrace, reached down, cupped her cheeks, and pulled her lips to his. The heat of their breath, their lips, merged into one.

Love battled logic and lost; Jill jerked out of the embrace, her nose wrinkled and a furrow beginning to form on her brow. "What's going on, David?" She grabbed her sore hand and pulled it behind her back, trying to stop it from shaking.

He looked at her, and Jill saw his familiar eyes sparkle. David. It's really David. His words broke her trance. "I don't have much time, Jill. I think I'm being followed. I know you are going to Istanbul. I'm going there too, just not by a public airline. I'll be there in two days. It's very sensitive right now. You have to be careful, Jill."

Jill didn't know how to process what David was saying. Was this even happening? Was this some apparition?

"Here." David pushed a note to her chest. "Meet me here in two days at nineteen hundred local time."

"But..." Jill stammered.

David stood strong. "Be careful, Jill. Don't tell anyone you've seen me. Make sure you are not being followed. I'll be waiting there. I'll be in the very back." Jill looked at the note and then back to David. "I have to go now, Jill." He pulled her back to him; his look was intense. The airport sounds became muted as if somehow paused. "I love you, Jill." And before she could respond, David turned and cautiously walked onto the sidewalk, camouflaging himself with the pace of the airport foot traffic. Jill spun fast and vomited.

CHAPTER SIX

The airline clerk studied Jill as he handed her back her boarding pass. Jill's eyes averted his studious stare, and she hoped the senior man couldn't smell her breath.

I vomited; I actually vomited.

Stomach gurgles, even twists and gut turns, were acceptable, but to Jill, puking was a sign of weakness, for God's sake. She kicked herself in the ass and moved down the jetway, onto the plane, and into her oversized seat. She'd made it.

The first leg of her journey from Tucson to Chicago was uneventful, and she now sighed in relief when the Boeing 777 hit cruise at 39,000 feet on its way to Turkey. "Newspaper? Magazine? Newspaper? Magazine?" the annoying flight attendant chirped.

The twelve-hour flight would at least be tolerable in business class. "Please, can you bring me a glass of red wine, cab sav if you have it?" Jill interrupted the attendant's routine and watched as he hurried off and was back in record time with an extra-large glass that would fit half a bottle of wine. The attendant poured a healthy amount into it as Jill continued her surveillance of her surroundings. Not knowing what she was looking for, Jill scanned for anything that looked out of place. She'd had a nagging feeling that she had been followed even after returning to Tucson—it was becoming a habit to scan her surroundings.

And then David.

What the hell! David is alive. Alive? Alive. She would compartmentalize this shocker right now. Because now, not only was he alive, but his warning weighed heavy on her. "I think I'm being followed. You have to be careful," he'd said.

Jill had no clue what the hell was going on, so she surveyed her space one more time. She looked to her right, then fifteen more degrees around her peripheral area, and then another fifteen degrees as if she were a magnet on a clock compass. Nothing appeared to be unusual. An experienced person following her would attempt to stay out of the 10 to 2 o'clock arc of Jill's immediate surroundings. Still, no one was suspicious on the flight unless you counted the older man who continued hacking before spitting up gobs into a handkerchief while looking directly at her. Jill didn't know if he disdained women or if he was physically or mentally challenged.

Her hand vibrated slightly as she attempted to raise the top-heavy wine glass and conceded to using both hands. With one hand on the stem and the other on the glass bowl, helping her to get her much-needed reprieve, Jill closed her eyes as the woody flavor went down and breathed deeply. Three deep breaths later, she felt something. Pulling to be mindful of her surroundings, she squinted one eye open and found the weird older man still staring at her. She lifted her glass mockingly, gave an air-cheers, and took another swig. This made him turn his head, and she watched as he fumbled the remote control.

She looked at her remote control and couldn't bring herself to begin any mind-numbing entertainment. She was already numb. It was time. She had no choice now. She thought of David. Alive. Yup, alive! The bastard was alive, and he hadn't told her for what ... six weeks! Jill took a rather unladylike swig of wine and tried to cull her anger. Sift through it. Get rid of it. Who was she kidding? Did David even care? Did his words—I love you, Jill—even ring true to her? Jill hadn't realized she was sneering until the flight attendant came by and asked if everything was all right. She thought about what he had said. "I wanted to tell you sooner. But it wasn't safe. It's still not safe." Why the heck wasn't it safe? And why the hell did it matter now, anyway? Was he trying to protect her?

Time passed with mulling thoughts. Jill took another swig and noticed she had already drained her glass. She punched the call button on the remote. This time, a female flight attendant approached. "More wine, please." The woman, dressed in a bright orange uniform with a brown apron, nodded, smiled, and turned, prancing to the galley.

Jill finally relaxed as her vice warmed her, moving into the compartment she had mashed closed when she was mourning David's death.

Jill's thoughts battled against her intuition. David's lack of communication had begun to fuel a new, unfamiliar, unsettling feeling. Where had he been these past few weeks? She thought of his face. She thought of his touch. Jill felt a much-needed smile begin to grow and push her cheeks up, making her squint. Jill could feel herself slowly cracking open the door to that compartment of her mind that kept her safe from feeling—feeling anything, really.

The flight attendant sprung back beside Jill's seat, interrupting her thoughts. The attendant placed a fresh glass of wine neatly on Jill's table. Jill tried to get back into her mind, into her weary questioning of David. She tried to return to the warm butterfly feeling she had minutes ago. But she couldn't. She knew she couldn't. After all the anguish she had felt these past few weeks, mourning the loss of his love and that feeling. That feeling. Well, that was the game that swirled around inside, wasn't it? Game? Her heart kicked, jump-starting her emotional ride. She needed to go into the intuitive tunnels of her mind as she often did when she was trying to wrestle with a problem. She wasn't prepared for it. Or maybe she was. Too much wine, she thought. She took another sip and found her mind moving into those speeding tunnels—riding the bobsled of thought, riding the wave. Feel, Jill, feel. Breathe, Jill, breathe.

Her journey began. Her mind flew fast, as if her hair flew back to the speed of her thoughts. Questions tugged. And tugged. And tugged.

Usually, when Jill had to make a decision or identify what she was not able to see or understand physically, she'd go deep in thought—deep into the tunnels. Jill spent most of her time in the intuitive tunnels of her mind. It's where she went to find answers, especially when profiling as a terrorist profiler for the U.S. Marshal Service. And when she got to her place, it went fast. Her thoughts were too quick for recognition as Jill tried to understand what she was missing—what she was trying to solve. Her mind would ping her out of her trance if something did not flow right—did not compute correctly—was out of order. Her ride would stop at that time, and a clear image would appear in her mind.

"Ouch." Her right arm was hit, pulling her out of the tunnels. The knock was hard and almost made Jill spill her wine all over her chest. Jill tensed as she sat up and looked around. The plane seemed eerily quiet, and the only movement she saw was the crusty older man who must have bumped her as he made his way down the aisle to the back galley.

Jill sat back and stared blankly at the dark screen. She closed her eyes again and tried to hit resume on her thoughts. Nothing. Damn, her tunnel ride was interrupted. But what did that matter? Nothing was coming through anyway. It had been that way ever since she thought David was dead.

"He's alive, Jill," she whispered to herself, probably for the fortieth time since she saw him several hours before. She tried to understand. She recalled the gnawing intel that haunted her these past few weeks. She couldn't imagine that David would risk himself—risk her—to commit treason. When she first saw David's name on Stan's now-confiscated documents, she considered this. It wasn't just rumblings that David was working with Stan Brown. She saw his name with her own eyes. There were other things too. First, David's name was still in the NOC database at the CIA. Leila had confirmed that. And there was no paper trail, no way to discover that David was, in fact, a double agent. No one was talking.

David.

Her emotions were knocking on that compartment door of her mind again, trying to flood in and flood the tunnels, take control, and wash away his sins. She had felt him when he held her at the airport. The smell of him was intoxicating. And Jill wondered if it was that intoxication that had jumbled her thoughts. She knew her feelings were real, and she hoped he was too. But did she know anything? Why hadn't he contacted her sooner? Why did he let her think he was dead? And why didn't Leila realize he was alive? Or maybe she did. Jill's gut pricked. None of it made sense.

"More?" a crisp male flight attendant asked, almost clicking his heels. He put her glass on his tray, and as if he were an orchestra conductor, he filled her glass again. She studied him. Was he trying to get her drunk? Was he the one who was following her? She saw his smirk when he nodded after pouring yet another half a bottle of wine into the glass before turning around.

She knew she was paranoid. Well, she thought she might be. Every-thing that had just happened was the perfect breeding ground for that all-too-familiar PTSD panic attack, like a freight train speed-ing towards her. "Stop! Just stop," Jill muttered. She interrupted her thoughts and looked up at the camera mounted on most planes at the back of each galley. The green light was solid, so she knew she was being recorded. If something sinister was going on with the flight attendant or that dirty older man, it was being recorded. Jill huffed deeply, took another sip, and set the wine glass down. She watched the legs of the fine vintage slowly seep back into the bowl of the glass.

She again began to weigh what she knew. She rehashed her thoughts over and over and over. She was going around in circles. It was the wine, she knew, or the lack of food in her belly after puking. She hadn't felt like eating anything else.

Jill thought about the clay numbers in the soft pouch that her grandmother had given her. It was tucked up into the overhead bin. She used them as tools when she Remote Viewed. But the plane was too busy to consider any Remote Viewing session. Besides, she wasn't looking for anyone or anything. She was just trying to understand her thoughts—understand what the hell was going on. It wouldn't be much help.

A thought knocked at her temple like a woodpecker. Why did Stan have David's wedding ring? How did Stan get it? Was he telling the truth that David had given it to him? There had to be more to it. And who was following David right now? Maybe it was the CIA, and maybe David was a traitor?

Jill sat forward, tapped on the seventeen-inch screen in front of her, selected the flight path map, and then pulled out the crumpled note David had given her.

Galata

Beyoglu Street

Istanbul

Backside of blue statue

1900

Two days wouldn't pass fast enough. "Not fast enough," she whispered.

CHAPTER SEVEN

Istanbul, Turkey

The sound of ringing made him choke out his last snort. The fat man hacked as he reached the nightstand and grabbed the phone. "It's after two a.m.," he grunted, growling phlegm as his words caught in his throat. He listened, looked at the large mirror above his head, and watched his jaw drop.

"This was not part of the plan," he said. "It's too soon. The timing is off. Who the hell gave the order!" He sat up and coughed again, attempting to clear his throat. The large stomach that made him appear ten months pregnant covered his hairy rat. He flung his stubby legs onto the floor. Two brown girls lying next to him stirred.

"This is bullshit!" he yelled, his American drawl pitched. "Who the hell do you have working for you? What! Laudman232?" He stood up fast. "This could ruin everything! Yes, of course, we need an emergency meeting. I'm on my way." He pressed the off button on the phone so hard it looked like he would break it apart.

"Ehhh." The girl with slanted eyes moaned. "Ehhh." She rolled over and opened her eyes as her drugged haze began to drain, and she looked at him.

He turned and looked at the stirring girls, leaned over, and slapped the moaning girl in the face. "Shut up, you stupid bitch." He hit her

again before pushing her hard onto the bed. "I'll deal with you later."
Fat rolls plopped as he shuffled out of the room.

CHAPTER EIGHT

Istanbul, Turkey

The Ataturk Airport in Istanbul was like a scene from a graphic war novel. Bullet holes had pierced the marble walls. Jill carefully watched her step as she walked through the bomb-torn terminal. She tried to avoid the fine shards of glass in small piles. Jill was third in line as military rangers escorted them off the plane. What the hell had happened? The aircraft was late coming in from holding high in the air. It continued loops until they had no choice but to land because of low fuel; the captain's voice crackled over the PA. He warned them that there was an attack at the airport, but the bad guys had been taken care of, and he said now the airport was secure.

Jill reached for her cracked-screen mobile, but without the swipe feature, she couldn't open her phone. Damn. She followed the line of tired travelers through customs as they made their way to baggage claim and exit. One thing was sure: she was happy when she saw the sign with her name in the hands of a little man who waited patiently for her delayed flight. She did her scans before getting into the chauffeured car, closing the door of the black Audi limousine.

The drive to her hotel seemed eerily quiet—too quiet if people were following her. She kept glancing backward as headlights bobbed, reflecting off the back of the front seat headrests as they drove. She saw flicks of the driver's eyeballs staring at her before returning to the road. Jill's right eye twitched as she saw the familiar bobbing lights and wondered if whoever was on their ass could see her if she turned around. She reached for her pack, grabbed her small makeup mirror, and held it up, trying to see who was behind them with such bright lights—another eye flick from the driver.

The glare was blinding in the small mirror as lights from the vehicle directly behind them saturated it. "Excuse me." No answer from the driver. "Excuse me," Jill persisted.

The blank-faced man flicked his eyes at her. "Yes, ma'am?"

"Is it normal for people to be following so close? This guy or whoever is behind us is quite close. Can you get off this road? Take your next right turn, please."

"But ma'am, that's—"

"Do as I ask, please. I will pay you more. Please, see up there." Jill pointed ahead through the windshield. "Turn right at the lights!"

"The light is red, ma'am. I will have to wait for the light to turn green."

Their car stopped, and Jill thought she heard a car door slam behind her. "Go. Go now!" Jill commanded in her I-mean-business voice. Jill's body was forced backward, pushing her against the seat as the man gunned the gas. Jill leaned up and twisted to watch what the car was doing behind her. There was no one moving outside of the dark-colored sedan. She could see a glow of a cigarette from the lone driver as they cornered the block and disappeared back into traffic.

Minutes later, they pulled up at the small hotel with no trace of the car. The room was tacky, not majestic like the ad in the hotel lobby claimed. A wall-size mirror reflected Jill, showing that she was tired. She considered her image and wondered if she was losing it. No one was following her. No one. Perhaps it was jetlag or the fact that she could not sleep on the flight. She lost almost a day on the trip and had just over twenty-four hours until she met with David. Maybe David was wrong that he was being followed. Jill shrugged inwardly. Right now, she didn't care. What she needed was sleep.

Embroiled in her conflict, she flipped the spout on the shower and felt resigned that she wouldn't find out much for the next twenty-four hours. Her clothes sat in a pile on the marble floor as the steam puffed above the glass doors. She thought of David as the hot rain hit her back. The last time they had played with each other was in the shower in the glass house back in Tucson. Even under the hot water, her nipples went hard. Heat moved between her legs as she washed herself, thinking of him. She didn't know how long she was in the shower before the water ran cold. "Shit." She slapped the lever off.

Jill toweled her short, bobbed hair. She missed her long straight locks, but she had no choice but to cut them off in Afghanistan. Jill looked into the mirror; her grey-green eyes twinkled with freshness. She smiled back at her image and was reminded she was exquisite—a distinctive Native American beauty.

She sat at the desk, pulled the laptop out of her bag, and plugged it into the wall with the converter she found in the desk.

Jill sat and stared at the screen. David had warned her not to communicate with anyone about seeing him or to tell anyone he was alive. How the hell was she supposed to do that? She wondered where David was right now, and she wished she was able to pick up her goddamn phone, call him, and just ask what the hell was going on. Jill thought of who she could call. She thought of Eric. Eric Wallace had been her boss and, more importantly, her friend. He'd told her he'd help her before they discovered convincing evidence that David was dead. Jill scoffed. It wasn't so convincing now, was it?

Jill's thoughts moved to Leila. She and Jill had worked hard togeth-er for a few short days investigating David's disappearance. Leila. Why had she interrupted Jill's thought about David? Something niggled.

Jill stood and opened the minibar and was relieved to find it fully stocked. She grabbed a cab-sav, pulled a chilled wine glass from the fridge, twisted it open, and poured. "Nice budget, Europol." Jill smiled to herself and took a gulp, filled her glass back up, and sat back down. Leila. She combed her memory for information. What was bugging her about Leila? Jill took a sip. The fact that Leila had shown up in Hamburg and had already run into Stan Brown in Brussels. No such thing as coincidences, Jill thought again.

She mulled over her thoughts, and with no resolve, she picked up the phone and dialed room service. She hadn't eaten on the plane; she was too unsettled for food. But now, after her hot shower—after her release and now with the negotiated settlement between her brain, her gut, and her intuition, she was famished. It was an intense negotiation. There was only one thing to solve. David. Could she trust David? It was a given that she couldn't. After all, he'd let her down. Let her down! That was an understatement. He'd let her suffer, which isn't what your loved one does to you. No matter what. No matter your job. No matter your family. No matter what. Well, that was how she settled her mind, closed the door on that compartment, and locked it with her imaginary lifeline key.

The Filipina lady who answered the phone gave a sing-song, "Yes, ma'am, sir, but we are all out of chicken and beef." Jill settled for the grilled samosas and couldn't quite understand what was in the filling as the sweet girl just chimed, "Yes, ma'am, sir." When Jill questioned her about the red wine and asked if it was a cab sav or merlot, she said, "Yes, ma'am, sir." Jill didn't care anymore and ordered both.

Jill picked up the envelope sent by Europol and pulled out the docket, flipped it open, and read it a second time. Simple stuff. Mainly logistics about her lodging. Day of rest tomorrow and a pick-up at 0730 hours the following day. Included in the envelope was a small mobile phone. Jill pressed hard on the power button and watched the screen of the portable light up.

She thought about how she felt when she first received the docket in Tucson. Fragile. "Screw that," she whispered as she dropped the papers and placed the phone down. She stared at the blank computer screen. David knew Jill had an assignment in Turkey. He said he was coming here too. "CIA bullshit," Jill surmised.

And that was all it took. One thought. Just one thought. The door to the locked compartment labeled "David" was buckling in on her. Jill fingered the mouse and clickily clacked her way to Google Maps, then reached over and looked at the crumpled piece of paper David had given her. She entered the hotel name of where she was staying and then the restaurant name where David had said to meet and wondered if Google had mapped Istanbul. A blue line formed, and the meeting place David had selected appeared to be at least five blocks from her hotel.

Jill leaned back and took a sip of wine. Who was she kidding? Why in the hell would she even consider meeting David, especially after her resigned decision about him? She cinched her robe, lifted her feet onto the desk, leaned back as far as possible, and closed her eyes. She breathed several yoga breaths and just let her thoughts come.

It was officially our first date. We didn't call it that; to this day, it was an ongoing razz between us. It was a hot August night, and we decided on Thai. As we sat eating Pandola's chicken at the local hole-in-the-wall in downtown Tucson, I decided right then. David was different. He didn't seem caught up in personal ambition or material achievements like most men I encountered. David appeared to cherish life—cherish living. It was as if he knew his destiny and enjoyed the journey toward it.

The heat was hot that night and wasn't from the desert weather. We sat sipping cab sav, getting to know each other. I watched him delicately cut his chicken into small pieces, then dip them in the spicy peanut sauce before opening his mouth, inserting his fork gently before slowly chewing. I could picture his mouth devouring me. It was hard to concentrate. But it wasn't his mouth that first intrigued me. His bright blue eyes and the energy from his pores that evaporated from the heat surrounded him with a beautiful blue aura—capturing me.

We sat, he telling me about himself and me telling him about myself. Us laughing. We talked for hours, but it seemed like minutes. We were consumed with each other, unconscious of the thoughts of the present. I could feel him feel me, and we hadn't even touched. It was as if a magic fairy had sprinkled us with lust dust, and it was all I could think about. I wanted him. As I watched him, I wanted to ravish his tight body, feeling his strength—feeling him. How I got him into my bed that night, I can't remember. I was too busy drinking his energy and wanting him inside me.

It was always that way with us. We could spend hours when he was home, lying in bed, looking at each other and not saying a word. And the magic fairy would come, sprinkling her dust, again and again, filling me—filling my soul. Bliss. Bang. Bang. Bang.

"Hello, ma'am. Hello, room service." Jill sat upright and listened, pulled her robe together, and cinched it tight as she walked over and opened the door. A little man scurried in, clipping the door open, and rolled a makeshift table in front of one of the chairs, clamping on the brakes with his foot before waving his arm for Jill to sit. "Enjoy, ma'am," he nodded, turned, unclasped the door, and left without so much as a tip.

CHAPTER NINE

The light of dawn tapped on the window of Jill's suite, trying to get her attention. She didn't notice. She was busy. She was watching what had happened at the Ataturk airport she had just entered. Several mainstream media channels reported the breaking news of a suicide bomb attack at the Istanbul airport. She tried to make sense of the truth of what had just happened in Turkey. Jill thought. She thought about a lot of things. She thought about the timing of her plane. She thought about the scheduled arrival time coinciding with the bomber's detonation. And she thought about what David had told her. David. She recalled that he said he'd arrive in Istanbul after she had. She felt relieved that her plane had not landed on time and blew on her coffee before sipping the hot liquid.

Her training had told her that the face of the bomber being splashed about was obviously some sort of coup. She considered how they could have known so fast who he was and the motive behind the media leak. If this happened in the US, Jill herself would have been called into the SOG operation center to review briefs and comb through databases to determine if this suspect had a history in the US. She'd be summoned to profile the shit out of him. When the news started replaying with no new stories, Jill closed her eyes and considered. Was it a coincidence that this happened? She did not know.

Her thoughts moved backward; she couldn't help it. It was true that she was still in love with David. Even if she couldn't admit it to herself, more glaring to her was that she also knew she couldn't trust him—wouldn't trust him. A sizzling image of one of their more passionate entangled moments crossed her mind. She smiled and crossed her legs. Several minutes passed as she doused her inner fire and clunked the cup on the table. "Stop it, Jill. Stop it!"

She knew she was on the last legs of jetlag, and she knew she needed sleep. She had almost fifteen more hours before she would see him again. She walked over, flicked off the main light, left the desk lamp on, headed to the bed, dropped her robe, and slid into the cool, crisp sheets. She pushed hard on the door called David. Pushed hard. Pushed hard...

The glass house sat on the foothills of the Catalinas, edging Tucson, Arizona. Jill stood before David's office door, listening to him talk on the phone. The door was closed. What did she hear? Who was he talking to?

Jill opened her eyes and ruminated about this vision. Ruminated. Suddenly she sat up. She remembered this day; it was the day that David had lied. It was the first lie she had caught him in. He had said he was speaking to his editor, Jeff. Jill had questioned him, and that was his response. To Jill, she felt that he was talking to a female. It was part of her BEA training, behavioral evidence analysis. She hadn't known then, not until Jill had met up with Leila, and she disclosed to Jill that it was Leila he was talking to that morning. Leila.

Jill flung the sheets off her, grabbed her robe off the floor, and marched to the desk. She reached into her bag that sat upright beside the desk and pulled out her notebook. She had reviewed her notes over and over in the past few weeks. She even scrutinized them with more vigor while on the plane. She was missing something. Jill knew she was.

This time, she didn't grab it to review her notes. This time, she turned to the next blank page, clicked on a pen, and added the date to the top. She wrote "Leila" in the middle of the page and then circled it.

Jill was a mind mapper. She used this powerful graphic technique to unlock the potential of what she was thinking and feeling. Anything that Jill thought of—word, image, number, logic, rhythm, color, and awareness—she'd write it down. She used this technique when profiling; more than ever, she needed to use it now.

She flipped back to a page in her notebook she had scribed several weeks ago on her journey to find David. It looked like a child had scribbled all over it. Doodles, words, and arrows filled the page. Then she saw what she was looking for. The word "family" was circled. When she had mind-mapped this page, her thoughts were about her family. She remembered the dreams she had had then. The dreams were about her mother and her grandmother. Family. Jill thought that was all it was about. Well, that was until she met up with Leila. It was Leila who suggested that the word family may not be about Jill's family, but David's—about Stan Brown. She turned back to the page with the lone word "Leila" and leaned back in her chair, staring blankly at it.

She knew that the image of David lying was significant. Images that were so vivid always were. She profiled herself with questions ... why was she even doing this? She began her journey back into the "tunnels." Her mind raced back to feel more images. More times. More. She remembered some of David's closed-door office calls, several in fact, just before the fateful trip to Doha, Qatar, where his colleagues last saw him—any one of them, for that matter. At that time, she blamed her suspicious mind, and maybe a little bit, just a little bit, she blamed her PTSD and her heightened senses, compliments of Mathew

McGregor. She didn't understand her over-the-top curiosity then. But now...

"Alfred Maxter. You are one sick puppy coming to my place. How the hell did he even know where I was staying?" She thought about this one little fact. She hadn't considered this until now. Their house had sold in just one day, and she was staying at an apartment hotel in downtown Tucson. It wasn't common knowledge. Or so she thought. Sure, the media had bombarded her upon her arrival from Dubai once they knew the missing journalist was David. They were all over the story. But the story soon died. "Just another lost journalist or military personnel fighting for their country. Page five news, then soon, no news. That suited Jill fine enough. Only Eric had known where Jill was staying. Well, Kali too. Kali Lucas had stopped several nights a week for wine time to solve the world's problems. Well, at least their problems. Jill knew she meant well. Babysitting her. But hey, that's what good friends do. After all, at that time, everyone assumed David was dead. But how the hell did that ambulance chaser know where to find her? And why hadn't he learned that David was dead? Now this knowledge intrigued her.

Who else? Jill thought of Leila and tried to remember if she had told Leila where she was staying. Then the image of Jill standing, listening to David behind a closed door that day several months ago, pushed its way back into Jill's thoughts. She was missing something. What the hell was it? The impact of this revelation sucker-punched her in the gut. She needed to call Eric. She needed to call Eric now.

CHAPTER TEN

Pelican Bay State Prison, Crescent City, California

The door of the interrogation room clanked shut behind Alfred Maxter. A tacky black fedora sat too high on his head in an apparent attempt to look younger. But the gray hair protruding under his hat dialed his age into the late fifties.

"Tell me!" Matthew grunted as metal chains pulled in and out of the one-inch metal loop that secured his wrists to the metal table. The green table was attached to the floor with two lag bolts on each leg.

Alfred croaked, "I, ah ... I ..." He examined the metal shackles that secured Matthew's ankles, scraped a metal chair across the concrete floor, and sat down. He had done this before, and now he knew better. He calculated the distance of the chains before looking at the two-way mirror. "I found her." His shoulders twitched as a bead of sweat bubbled below the rim of his hat.

Matthew jolted forward; the cuffs of his restraints clanked on the metal table.

Alfred knew he was far enough away, but he couldn't stop the slight tremble in his bottom lip. "She was on her way to the airport. I, ah... well, she blew me off." A slow-motion sneer began to form on Matthew's face. Alfred's words rambled fast. "Why is this so important? Why do you need to reach her so badly? It's not as if you

can profit from this book. Frankly, I doubt she'd consider coming at
all. After all ..." Alfred trailed off as he could swear that with every
word he spoke, Matthew's eyes would narrow and narrow and narrow.
And yes, he wasn't imagining it. They narrowed one last time before
Matthew's lip curled as he shot a look at the two-way mirror. Alfred
knew, and he knew Matthew did too, that whoever was behind it could
only see them, not hear them—new privacy laws after the Snowden
fiasco. Matthew turned. His eyes widened; he smiled and let out a
hiccupped giggle.

"It's none of your business; it's family business. Blood business."
Matthew leaned back, his demeanor changing again. "Did you get
the authorization from my lawyer?" Alfred nodded. "The sentencing
is over, so I keep anything that is not valuable to the prosecutor."
Matthew grinned a broad smile that nearly cracked his cheeks. Seconds
passed as Matthew studied his biographer. "Get the box, Alfred. Get
the box from where I told you it is, and do not open it."

"What's in the box? I don't want to take part in any crime." Alfred
hesitated and said, "You know I can't be part of any offense." His hands
had a slight tremble, and he quickly pushed them under the table,
attempting to squeeze the nervousness out.

Matthew's face began to twist into something unrecognizable,
and he lowered his head. A minute of huffing had passed before a
high-pitched, grumbling, smoker-like voice spat in a different octave.
"Do as the boy says, Alfred, or you'll be a bad boy, and you know what
happens to bad boys."

Alfred stood fast. The chair clattered as it flew backward, hitting the
tile floor. Matthew lurched forward. Saliva spewed from his mouth as
he growled, "Find Jill Oliver, Alfred. Find my sister now!"

CHAPTER ELEVEN

Jill pulled open the curtains and squinted at the midday sun as it attempted to cheer up the room. She left a message after several attempts to reach Eric, to no avail. She lifted the hotel room coffee pot, then put it back in its cradle. She looked at the coffee basket and knew she would not get another cup without finding housekeeping or pinching one from an unmanned maid's cart in the hallway. Jill turned as she heard the familiar sound of incoming email notifications. When she clicked on the bright green video mail icon, a new pop-up window opened and began to load a streaming video. Curly red hair filled the screen in a Medusa-like fashion.

"I hope you made it there in one piece. Please call me as soon as you can." The vmail closing sounded as if a black hole was swallowing it. Kali was bragging now about sending this type of message. She had rambled on about this new technology they had been testing for some time. But hearing Kali's voice made Jill smile.

Jill glanced at the clock, decided that Kali should still be in the office, and clicked on her phone icon on her computer. "Hi," her voice drawled. "When did you get there?"

"A few hours ago. I was a bit busy, and well, it might just take longer for your email to arrive since it's in video format," Jill said mockingly.

"Nope, it's nanotechnology," Jill could picture Kali's smile as she retorted.

"I've been trying to call your mobile like twenty-seven hundred times, but it's been off, Jill. I'm so glad you finally called in. I knew your plane had arrived okay—gotta love my security clearance—but still, the bombing of the airport was extensive, according to the reports I've been able to access. And nothing further since you landed. Tell me, what did you see? What was it like? I mean... you know. Anyway, glad you are okay. Where are you staying? Will this new terrorist event take you away from your assignment?"

Jill glanced at the docket and thought of telling Kali about David. It wasn't a leap of faith by any means. She trusted Kali. "I'm staying at Sultan Hotel in Beyo something or other in Istanbul," she said while simultaneously considering what to do. Kali continued updating office gossip as Jill's mind wandered back to the nagging thought of what David had told her. Tell no one. Jill chose to keep the jury out on David at bay. Besides, right now, the less Kali knew, the better. She'd explain to Kali later why she could not disclose that she knew David was alive. Jill could imagine her words. "I'm going to kick your ass to the moon for not telling me, Jill!"

"... and Tom, you'll never guess. Yup, he found a girl that would date him. And no, he didn't have to pay her before you ask." Kali laughed. Silence. "Ummm, Jill? Jill."

"I'm here."

"Sorry, I know you don't need me to clog you up with the catch-up. You must be tired?"

Jill looked over at the grandiose gold and red velvet bed. "A little."

"Okay, I won't keep you, but I had a situation I thought you should know about." Hearing the word situation made Jill stiffen. She knew what was coming next. "It's Matthew McGregor." Jill winced at the sound of his name. "He ... well ... remember he tried to reach you when you were in Afghanistan? Well, that author dude, anyway."

"When was this? The twerp came to my apartment as I left to come here."

"Your apartment? But..."

"Yeah, someone must have told him where I was staying. But very few people knew this detail."

"Totally weird. He must have called here after meeting you, as it was only a few hours ago. I am still determining how he found you. He didn't mention that he saw you when he called. What he said was odd, though. What did he say to you?"

"I didn't give him a minute of my time; I was late for my flight. And even if I wasn't, odd? What do you mean, odd?"

"He said he needed to speak to you and that it was urgent. What could be pressing from a writer?" Kali said rhetorically. "Anyway, he said he has been interviewing Matthew and desperately needed to disclose his discovery to you before the book is published. Something about rights and all. Or at least that's what he said it was about."

"That's stupid," Jill spat. "He just wants more meat for his story. He wants to sell more books. If he calls again, tell him I told him he can go to hell."

Silence hogged the digital line before Kali continued. "Umm, okay, Jill. It's just... it's just that he sounded so desperate. Guess I'm Gordie Gullible these days. He said he was going to keep trying himself. As if he could find you in Turkey, and definitely not now with all the mayhem there. Anyway, no worries. Get some rest and stay safe."

Jill clicked the phone off and looked over at the bed. She conceded again for the second time today. She crawled back under the crisp sheets and sighed. She thought about Matthew. She thought about

his trial. She thought about the high-security lockdown he was in at
Pelican Prison. "Stop it! Stop it!" she hushed as her heavy eyes closed.

"Drip. Drip. Drip." Jill rolled over in her bed and covered her head
with her sheets. Except there were no sheets. There was no bed. "Drip.
Drip. Drip." She slowly opened her eyes. Blackness. She tried to move,
realizing her knees were tucked tight to her chest, and she was in
the fetal position. She reached out with her right hand, trying to feel
around her. Nothing. The niggle in her brain forced her out of her fog
and pricked her belly. Where was she? Why was it so dark—so cold?
Her hands moved fast, skimming her body for signs of trauma. What
she discovered was that she was naked. Is this a dream?

Cement pushed hard on her back, and she suddenly jolted up. Her
eyes began to adjust to the blackness. Jill squeezed her lips tight and
held her breath when she heard the sound again. "Drip. Drip. Drip."
She huffed out a breath and tried to get her bearings. A sliver of light
beamed in from an unknown source, growing in slow motion, lighting
up what Jill recognized as a jail cell. She blinked as her brain wave
connected. Jill stood fast, ran to the bars, and frantically tried to shake
them. "Help. Help me." The cell door rattled but gave no relief or
opening. Jill fumbled from bar to bar, trying to find the door at a
frantic pace. "I... eh... I... Help!" She shook the bars and screamed as
she sank to the floor.

It was only a minute that passed when she heard something. "Oh,
Jillllll!" he sing-songed and stood directly before her.

Jill's head began to spin like an out-of-control tilt-a-whirl. Her
vision began to narrow, closing as she saw Matthew. The ringing in her
head sounded like an old-fashioned telephone. Ring-ring. Ring-ring.
Ring-ring...

Jill sprang upright and looked around the room. Ring-ring. Ring-ring. Ring-ring. Her body was covered in sweat as she reached over to the phone on the bedside table. "Hello? What? Matthew!"

CHAPTER TWELVE

The day had sped by faster than Jill imagined it would. Most of it was spent in and out of jetlagged sleep. Jill had finally found deep sleep after her dream of Matthew. The phone call from the front desk had rattled her internal cage. How strange was it? Someone calling was asking for Matthew. It wasn't Matthew McGregor, of course. The receptionist had called the wrong goddamn room. She determined this little reality after she was fully awake. The dream was more vivid than any she had ever had about Matthew McGregor, and for that, she excused her fearful response.

One thing for sure nagged at Jill all day, and this thought kept her tossing and turning: Eric. It was the first thought that crept into her mind when she awoke from her long sleep. Eric had not called her back. Eric had yet to email her back. She contemplated calling Kali to see if she knew where he was, but it was nighttime in the States. She'd have to wait it out. She knew he'd call back soon. And frankly, she didn't even know if her theory made sense anymore after she had gotten some rest. But something was amiss about it; that much she knew. Besides, she was consumed with the present—her present. It was an all-out battle with herself. The big, life-changing question: you guessed it, David. What would she do when she saw

David? Jill walked out into the chilly night, happy she had had more than a few hours to contemplate how she felt about him again. Was she overreacting? Surely she was. But what he did was cruel—not letting her know he was alive. Jill wondered if he had watched her in Tucson—watched her suffer. She wondered, too, if he had gotten her voicemails. She'd left him one every day when she got back to Tucson. The pain of never hearing from him again was all too much. Kali was the only one she confided in about her brokenness—her anguish. She hadn't heard from Leila since she first got back to Tucson. She surmised then that Leila was like all of the other friends of David's; they turned out to just be colleagues. But if that was the case, that Leila was not her true friend but just a former colleague of David's, why pick at a scab and tell Eric her theory? Jill sighed and thought about Kali. The guilt began to trickle down to her gut. She thought about Matthew McGregor and his thorny author showing up on her doorstep, but that thought was pushed away by the thought of Leila again. Although the night was chilly, sweat began to form on her upper lip. It was a sure sign that she was well aware of. She knew a panic attack was coming; she'd felt it many times over the years.

She thought about what her psychologist had said during therapy three years ago, after McGregor... after hell. Usually, after repressed memories begin to surface, PTSD can creep in. And her dream was just that. "There are varying degrees of it. It depends on you, Jill, how your level of trauma affects your ability to cope. You will probably never forget what happened to you and may not fully remember everything. But I promise, if you can learn what to do and how to handle these returning memories, then, as I said, that's fifty percent of the battle to overcome any lingering PTSD symptoms."

Now, she needed to breathe. "Just breathe!" If she could catch it in time, it would pass. Jill stood for a moment, taking deep yoga breaths, attempting to compartmentalize Matthew McGregor—compartmentalize herself and all her bouncing thoughts. She stood in front of the hotel and breathed and breathed and breathed. She sucked in the night air and huffed out the panic.

Several minutes passed, and she knew she had won this battle round. Jill looked around and wondered if anyone had witnessed her near meltdown. There was no bellhop at the door like there had been when she arrived. Jill spotted the only taxi parked at the curb. It looked clean, and a neatly dressed Black man sat behind the wheel; he was watching her, and when he caught her gaze, he waved her over.

"You need a taxi?" he said in broken English.

Jill gave a half-smile, opened the door, and slid across the plastic seat. "I need to go to Galata Restaurant. It's about five blocks from here." The man nodded and sped out of the hotel driveway.

The taxi bumped over two sets of tracks, cutting in front of the bright red streetcar before crossing a pedestrian lane and merging onto the main road.

It only took a few minutes to get through two sets of lights before Jill recalled the Google map she had studied earlier and figured they should have turned left at the last light. After that, a second right. But the taxi driver kept going straight. Jill examined the man's identification picture that hung next to the meter and then his name. Then back to the image. The photo displayed a brown-skinned man with bright blue eyes. This was not the man who was driving this taxi. Her situational awareness kicked in hard, and Jill began her scan. They were going slower than the other cars on the three-lane road. It was busy, but perhaps he was giving her the tourist route so he could earn more money for the fare.

"Excuse me," Jill said pointedly. "Shouldn't you be turning left?" As she said this, she felt her body push back from the taxi's acceleration, going straight through another set of changing lights. Dark, cold eyes looked at Jill from the rearview mirror. It was the blank look in them that caught her attention. She'd seen that blank stare before. She knew. Jill knew she had to get out of the taxi, and she knew she had to get out now.

Ahead, the green light began to flash, indicating that it would turn yellow, then red. A large lorry painted in a splattering of different colors was on the right. A smaller truck carrying goats directly ahead of them braked for the changing lights. The taxi lurched to a stop, and the driver impatiently began honking the horn. Beep, beep, beep, the little cab burped. His hands smacked the steering wheel.

Jill looked down to the left, trying to locate the door handle. There was none. Looking over to the right door, she spied its handle. But if she jumped out of the car, she might get struck by the large lorry braking. No time to stop, no time to think. Jill's butt slid fast; she grabbed the handle and yanked. Nothing happened. "Ahh!"

She had pulled several times before the taxi driver turned in her direction. His brown teeth pushed out the words. "You cannot escape, Miss Oliver."

Survive. It was just one word. The one word gave her strength for what she instinctively did next. There wasn't enough space for a full-force roundhouse kick, so she grabbed the door armrest on her left with both hands for leverage, shifted her weight to the left side of her body, and swung her leg with all her strength counterclockwise over the front passenger seat. A solid crack to the side of his head sent it sideways. Teeth splattered against the windshield as the toe of Jill's boot connected with his jaw. The driver bounced forward; his head tapped on the horn as he slumped. Jill wriggled over to the front seat. She crawled over him, crushed his face further against the steering wheel, reached for his door handle, and yanked it. As the door fell open, she tumbled out onto the ground. Her fingers bit into the pavement as she scrambled to her feet—a cacophony of horns orchestrated around her from impatient drivers as the light turned green.

Adrenaline surged as cars honked past her, and she navigated across the busy road. She reached the opposite side and got her bearings before ducking around a building, bringing her onto a back street. Several buildings down and across the alley blinked a sign: Café.

The waft of cigarette smoke made Jill gag as she sat down on the rattan chair hidden in the back area of the shop. She pulled out her new mobile. Who was she kidding? She didn't know who to call. But she swiped her phone open anyway. Contacts. Empty. Then Jill recognized the 3G symbol and tapped the Google Maps app. A man approached in casual clothes. "Coffee?" Jill nodded and wiped her forehead with the napkin he had placed on the table. She typed "Galata Restaurant" into the mobile app. She glanced at the time: 19:10. She watched the familiar red dot pulse and hit the direction button. The green dot blipped, signaling Jill's phone location at the café. A blue line began to route the directions to the restaurant. She was right about the direction she was supposed to be going when she confronted the taxi driver. She was only one block away. She studied the map and zoomed into street view. She needed to go. She needed to go now.

She couldn't trust another taxi, at least not on her own. And how the hell did he know her name? David? Jill stood and moved towards the door of the café.

Reaching it, she paused and did her scans. She hadn't realized the backside of the café was on a brightly lit street. Colorful lights danced on the side of the building in the wind. Large blinking signs with the word "tattoo" checkered each building on the street, reminding her of a carnival fair. She needed to get off this exposed road. She glanced back at the mobile app and was about to walk out the door when she heard a man's stern voice.

"Stop," the waiter said abruptly. Jill stiffened and slowly turned towards him. "You must pay." The waiter held up his hand, turned it with the tips of his fingers upwards, and tapped the ends together. "Shway. Shway."

Jill pulled out an American dollar bill and handed it to him. He grabbed it fast, turned, and plunked the coffee down, upcycling it onto a busy table.

Jill stood in the doorway and looked at the mini-map. She knew if she crossed the street directly in front of her, then made a right down that side street over there, she'd be less noticeable. Jill did her surveillance again. To her right, down the road towards the tattoo alley, throngs of men sat gathered in small groups at little café tables on the sidewalk. To her left, a crisscross of a busy intersection, and Jill wondered if it was the road she was initially on. She crossed the street rapidly, then took another right onto the side street. She followed the blue line; she looked for the indicator of when to turn. Her mind was racing now; she was too busy to enter the tunnels. Too busy saving her ass to do much of anything except find David.

But who was this taxi driver who knew her name? Who else knew she was in Turkey? Europol, of course. A niggle rattled a thought. Why hadn't she heard from them? Surely the reception of providing a driver wasn't their only intended contact with her. She found it weird when all that was in the envelope was an itinerary for tomorrow and this empty Turkish phone. Surely they would have had a brief for her to review? Jill shrugged off the thought and conceded. Why would anyone from Europol try to hold her against her will? The driver of the taxi had said she could not escape. Why would she need to escape? It must have something to do with David. It had to. Her boots crunched on the light gravel as she glanced again at the phone. The cold night air dried Jill's lips as fast as she licked them.

David said he was involved with her assignment here. Would he know where she was staying? What the hell was going on? Jill was a Crime Analyst, for goddamn's sake. A pencil pusher. She'd had enough of this cloak-and-dagger bullshit when she traipsed halfway around the world to find David. In Afghanistan, of all places. Jill remembered the man she'd shot in the gunfight in Kushka, Afghanistan. It haunted her; she'd never killed anyone before. But she had no choice. Then Zayed was dead. Then Zayed was alive. She remembered the men with Tasers in Germany. She remembered Stan Brown. She remembered it all. Now what the hell kind of crap was happening here in Turkey? She was pissed off now, and more than ever, she was determined to drop-kick David in the gut before telling him to get the hell out of her life forever. This thought stung Jill as soon as it crossed her mind. She should take it back. But one thing she had learned about herself at a young age was that she had zero tolerance for liars.

Jill continued her journey, glancing at the map. Matthew McGregor interrupted her mind. Then thoughts of her mother crept in—her mother, of all people. Matthew was trying to get in touch with Jill. It's what her therapist said would re-trigger her PTSD. She had put Matthew at bay when she met David. It was all coming back now. It was coming back all too fast.

But before she could give way to another oncoming panic attack, and before she could think about the brutal serial killer and how he had her hanging naked on a rail only three years earlier, she had to stop this from happening. She had to prevent a full-blown attack. She had to communicate; she had to survive. Shoot. Move. Communicate. Survive.

"Stop it," Jill muttered, pulling up the collar of her black coat as she turned the corner. She walked just briskly enough not to draw too much attention to herself. Intuition tapped her shoulder. Suddenly, Jill ducked into a covered doorway on the right. Instinctively, her right hand reached down her leg. No gun. She'd worn her snub nose in a pocket holder for the last several weeks in Tucson. She had usually kept it in the bedside drawer. When she returned from Abu Dhabi and was tying up loose ends—selling the house, her furniture, and her life—she'd felt it then too. Someone was watching her. Eric had thought it was the rogue Chechens, but she didn't know for sure, even after a hit on his search about them. David. He was in her head again. Maybe she felt him watching her. David must have been following her in Tucson. Suddenly, this thought was interrupted by a car crawling up the road.

Jill ducked into a doorway and pressed her back hard against the wall. There was just enough shadow from the streetlights to cover her. Gravel crunched under the tires as it inched closer.

And Jill had no gun. If they stopped, she'd have to do something. Think, Jill. She had the weapon of surprise. And she could run—run like hell. The sides of the tires popped pebbles as they pulled alongside the doorway.

CHAPTER THIRTEEN

Steam rose from the newly poured American coffee. David blew on the hot brew, then took a light sip as he scanned the restaurant. The low-lit bar looked like it belonged on a posh African safari. Its bright red walls punched against the zebra-patterned chairs. David had already noted the entry and various exits—standard operating procedures in the spy world. He had even counted how many steps to the fire escape and chosen the table with the best view of the restaurant and its occupants. He looked for possible hostiles, but David identified none.

He glanced at his watch for the eighth time in the last five minutes. Jill was late. In Turkey, that didn't mean much. But David knew that one of Jill's quirks was always being on time. He had been thinking about her this whole trip. When he saw her at the airport, something leaped inside him. Maybe her beauty. Maybe. Anguish seeped through his veins like fluid through an IV. How could he have been so obtuse as to allow the CIA and its rules to stop him from letting her know he was alive? That was unkind, even for him. Sometimes he wondered how he had even gotten into this situation. Should he have just stayed a NOC? He did not know the answer.

David lifted his head when the humidity fogged in from the opened door and watched as two men dressed in black army fatigues walked in. They began to scan the restaurant. David knew instantly this was not good. They must be looking for him—followed him; otherwise, how would they know he would be at this same restaurant? No one knew he was here except Jill.

David stood and slowly moved behind the cover of the stone pillar blocking their view of him. He calculated that they would make their way to him in about thirty-eight seconds. David turned and moved quickly in the direction of the back exit. Too quickly. His shoulder briefcase nudged the top of a chair as he passed, and that was just enough to catch the attention of one of the men. David rushed to the back exit door and pounded the bar before entering the night. He was in some courtyard. David didn't have time to calculate. He had to move. He ran to one of the tall stone walls and jumped. His hands gripped the top of the wall; the momentum helped him swing his left leg up fast. He hooked his left foot and pulled himself up. Just before he jumped over the wall, a bullet shot past his head.

CHAPTER FOURTEEN

The black SUV coasted past Jill, who was holding her breath. The windows were tinted, and she couldn't see inside. She did not move. She held her breath. She stiffened when the brake lights blinked on. Jill bolted from the safety of the doorway and sprinted across the road. Gravel spat as the SUV roared, fishtailing as it attempted a reverse cop turn. The sound of her boots smacked the ground as she tried to find another way to get off this street. Ahead, as if appearing from nowhere, a small back alley emerged. It was behind a pile of garbage and was too small for any car. Whoever was chasing her would have to follow on foot. Jill ducked to the right and into the alley. The smell of garbage punched her in the nose. A cat screeched as it jumped out of her way. The lane began to swell with rusty tin walls and electrical wires. She could see a light about twenty yards ahead that appeared to be a busy street. Jill slowed to an accelerated walk as she approached the end of the alley and looked back over her shoulder. No one was trailing her. No one was there. Even in the dark alley, she would have been able to see the movement or hear the sounds of someone following her.

She stopped at the end of the lane, her breath starting to slow. She peered down each side of the street. Nothing seemed out of the ordinary. People were walking to and fro. She didn't have time to do her scans. She had to move. She turned right and walked with a purposeful gait, a little faster than some pedestrians. She didn't know exactly where she was, but Jill guessed she must be close to where she was supposed to meet David. She wanted to stop and pull out her mobile to look at Google Maps, but she had to keep moving. Who was Jill kidding? She needed some help. She needed some directions. She needed a break. She pulled out her mobile phone and swiped. The blue light blinked, and Jill edged into the next alley and tried to get her bearings.

Her intuition began to rumble in her gut. Strong arms wrapped around her torso from behind, pinning her arms. Jill did what any woman would do if she were trained in self-defense. She immediately straightened her arms, jolting them away from her chest fast enough to make the man's arms flinch, keeping him off balance—distracting him. And then Jill made her move. She only needed a split second, and she took it. She punched her heel down hard and attempted to crack his foot. It was a classic maneuver. But she made one mistake—she miscalculated and missed. He pulled back hard, and his bear hug would not budge this time. She was about to kick her feet, trying to hurt the strong man. Then, her mind connected to her senses. It was the smell of David.

CHAPTER FIFTEEN

Jill stopped fighting. "David?" She was tense as David released his grip on her. Jill turned fast, pushing his hands back hard. "Get your hands off me." David lifted his index finger and pressed it to his lips. "What...?" Jill turned 360 degrees, doing her scans. She could see nothing.

"Come on," David whispered, pulling her towards him and around the corner of a dilapidated building. Turning their backs to the rickety tin structure, David continued, "Someone was following me. They shot at me."

"Someone was following me too, and he knew my name," Jill hushed. "Well, I guess being held captive in a taxi isn't exactly following me."

"What do you mean he knew your name? Who is he?"

Jill described what happened.

"Shit," David barked, grabbing Jill's arm at the elbow. "Let's go."

They moved in unison along the dark alley, then onto a quiet street. An SUV turned onto the road, and they ducked into another side alley. They crouched when they heard a slow-moving car and watched it pass. A flame flicked on as the man in the passenger seat lit a cigarette. There were two men inside. "Who are they?" Jill whispered.

"I'll explain later. We've got to keep moving," David said as he stood.

Jill turned towards him. "Explain now, David!" she said sharply.

"Listen, Jill, it's complicated. Too complicated to discuss here, right now." David looked past Jill over her shoulder, and Jill turned to watch the SUV make a second pass before the brake lights blinked on. Jill whirled around, and then David grabbed her arm. "Move," he said, pulling her as two car doors slammed.

They were running hard. At the end of the alley, David released Jill's arm. "This way." They dodged past two white Corollas, crossed a street, and ducked into another alley. Jill stumbled over a mound of what she hoped was just dry garbage before spilling onto the next street. It was busier than the last two streets. Cars beeped past them. A large blue sign blinked: Novotel Hotel.

Inside the lobby, Jill followed David to the sign that read Nov'ist. Jill coughed when she hit the wall of cigarette smoke entering the lounge. It was almost empty. Several men were watching an Eastern European woman with long, greasy blonde hair. She was dressed in a short pink skirt and a bright red tank top and mumbling. She had clearly had too much to drink—or too much of something. "Me give you happy ending," she slurred, stumbling.

They moved to a dark corner, and David pulled out his mobile phone and dialed. "This is Brown 2422203; we need extraction. Novotel, we're hot." He was listening when he looked around, getting his bearings on his surroundings. His surveying stopped on the red-painted sign that must have read emergency exit in Turkish. David nodded towards Jill, his phone still to his ear as they swiftly approached the exit door. "Ten-four," David said into the phone before body-checking the door and bursting into the night.

CHAPTER SIXTEEN

The SUV vibrated as it drove over the cobblestone. On the right was a long cement building. The doors were spaced every twenty feet apart, indicating there were several tiny row houses equally lining the street. You couldn't distinguish each home on the row except for the different colored doors.

"You can call me Fred. My name is not that, but call me Fred anyway," the driver said as they slowed on the quiet street. "Here we are, nice and safe, mate. We use this safe house now and again. It's not the Plaza, but you'll be safe here."

No identifying features made the house distinct, unlike its neighbors, which had brightly colored pink and green doors. Somehow these colors reminded David of the vibrant home of glass that Jill and he had shared in Tucson. He expected the house to sell slower. Otherwise, he would have done something to alert Jill he was there—still alive. But maybe he wouldn't have if he'd known. They stopped in front of one of the blander-colored doors painted the same color as the cement. If you didn't know the door was there, you might have missed it.

"Safe house?" muttered Jill as she took her bag from the man who called himself Fred. He just nodded. David took one look at Jill and immediately knew she was pissed off. Jill was beautiful to David and nearly any man who met her, even with a scowl on her face. Her new look with her short bob cut made her look more intriguing than her previous long-haired Pocahontas style. But it wasn't her hair that had him focused. It was the scrunched-face-death look that stopped his admiration. He had seen this look before when she was angry about something important.

David studied Jill. In the brief Paul had given him, he had read that Jill was instrumental in Stan's capture, but was she? David had received word to go to a small airport in the desert in a town called Al Ain in the Emirate of Abu Dhabi, United Arab Emirates. There were seven Emirates in total, including the Emirate of Dubai. It was just a short distance from where he'd last seen Zayed. His orders were clear: get out of Abu Dhabi. Get out of the UAE. Get out now. These orders and the capture of Stan Brown by the Abu Dhabi police all seemed to happen within hours.

His thoughts were interrupted when David noticed Jill doing a surveillance scan as she stood in front of the dingy villa. He hadn't seen her do that before. This single movement of Jill's brought David back to the discussion of Jill with his case officer, Paul. Remote Viewer, he thought to himself. He stared at her and wondered who Jill really was. She seemed different from the woman he married in Tucson just over a year ago. One year. He hadn't planned for that period of time. Plan? Everything goes differently than planned.

The main door was two steps into a cobblestone lane doorway. Fred made a series of swipes on his phone, and the deadbolt lock automatically turned. He showed David the phone as he pushed the door open, spouting a series of numbers as he tapped it to disengage the alarm.

"There's a camera here." He pointed at the doorbell. "You can see who is at the door from anywhere in the world and unlock it, too, if it's safe." Fred continued giving the tour and walked inside. "If anyone comes to the door, the movement starts the camera to record."

Another swipe of the phone turned on the interior lights. In front of them was a long, brightly lit, cement-walled hallway. David motioned for Jill to go in ahead of him, then turned as Fred swiped the deadbolt closed behind him. "There's a fully stocked fridge, mostly canned crap to microwave and some drinks to take the edge off," Fred continued as he followed them through the safe house.

The first room on the left was a living area. Inside, the small room was cramped. Two couches hugged a solid wood coffee table.

"You'll like this." Fred smiled with glee. He bent over the table, flicked a metal clasp on its side, and pulled open the top. Inside were several weapons and boxes of ammunition.

Jill walked over, lifted the Sig Sauer P226, and released the magazine into the palm of her hand. "Thirteen," she said as she studied the magazine.

"Now, now, little lady. Be careful with that." Jill gave the man called Fred a you're-dead-to-me look, stuffed the magazine back into the gun, then placed the gun down.

"Wished it had the red-dot sight. I always kill better with that." She glared at Fred, then turned and walked out of the room.

David shrugged, admiring Jill as she went back into the hallway. It was that grit that intrigued David when he first met her on a rafting trip on the Colorado River. And David found her in her office three weeks later—he went there unannounced. At first, she seemed annoyed that he had just shown up, but that soon passed. Even then, that annoyance made him smile.

But it was her sensual beauty that captured his heart in bed. Her native skin, tight on her fitness-model body waiting for him to investigate—to explore. Her tight chest had just enough for him to cup in his hands, just enough for him to hold tight as he fingered-flicked, then licked her nipples. It captivated him that even though she had a solid alpha-female personality, she had a feminine and vulnerable side in the sack. She always wore dainty, laced panties. He would slowly kiss her belly, moving down towards her crotch. He'd start by kissing the seam above her pelvic bone, slowly moving her legs apart, then pecking her inner thighs towards the prize. Gently pulling at its seam with his teeth, pushing them out of the way, he'd suck her luscious fruit before plunging his tongue inside her. Jill wouldn't take long to thrash before using some martial arts move with her legs, flipping him onto his back and grabbing his wet lips with her teeth. Then she would submerge herself on top of him, bucking him deep inside her.

"Where do we sleep?" Jill called from the hallway, interrupting David's thoughts. Fred grumbled something unrecognizable and pushed past David into the hallway.

David adjusted himself, and before leaving the living area, he scanned the room. For the first time, he noticed something peculiar. The chalk-white walls had no windows.

David walked up behind Jill as she stood at the open bathroom door. Fred moved past them. David glanced in, leaning over her shoulder. "Doesn't look too bad," he said. The bathroom tile was prison-cell gray. A shower stall, a toilet, and a sink blended with the same color.

He rested his hand on Jill's shoulder before she shrugged it off and said, "Right."

Fred pointed towards two doors at the end of the hall and said, "And here, ladies and gentlemen, we have the deluxe suites." They looked in each room one by one. They were identical. The navy-blue bedding on two small single beds was pulled tight.

"There are no windows," David said. "There are no windows in the living room either."

Fred looked at David and nodded. "Yup. The only way in or out is through those doors." He pointed back down the narrow hall to the front entrance. "I'm told to tell you to stay put until you hear from him." He passed the phone to David. "He'll call you on that phone. Hand me your other one."

David reached into his pocket, pulled out his disposable phone, and held it up. "Look, man, it's untraceable."

Fred reached over, grabbed the phone, and dropped it to the floor before crushing it with his foot. "You can never be too careful." He moved towards the door, manually unlocked it, and said, "Lock it," before shutting the door behind him.

CHAPTER SEVENTEEN

Somewhere in a brothel, Istanbul, Turkey

Water dripped in the pipes somewhere, and Gabby tried to listen to it—to think about it, wonder where it might be, take her mind off the pain.

Pain everywhere. The haze of drugs was beginning to wear off. Her body was damaged—she was damaged.

But as her mind returned to her, she remembered she knew how to deal with the pain—the toe trick.

Gabby focused on the big toe of her right foot. She imagined a needle—sharp, glistening—penetrating under the toenail. It hurt like nothing she'd ever experienced. A needle hammered underneath the nail. Again. And again. And again.

Her right toe throbbed. Her eyes fluttered open, and she stared at the cracks in the ceiling. That was better. All the pain in one spot. Easier that way.

When would they send another man in? There were always more. A never-ending stream of customers. Gabby closed her eyes and tried to force her mind back to her toe, but the thought crept in anyway.

What would her mother say if she could see Gabby like this?

A hollow ache began in Gabby's chest when she pictured poor Mama's face. How long had it been since Mama died? It must've been at least a few months since cousin Arianne had sent her to this "boarding school."

Some boarding schools.

Gabby could still picture Arianne through the van's back window, growing small in the distance, counting bills of money. Money Gabby now understood was for her. Mama died, and cousin Arianne had sold her.

The hollow ache inside grew.

Had her thirteenth birthday passed yet? No, it hadn't been that long, surely. She was still twelve. Twelve years old and far away from home.

Would she ever see Italy again? What about the birthplace she could hardly remember—Tennessee? Or would she be stuck in this strange place forever where the mistress of the house hugged and beat her in turns, where everyone shouted at her in Turkish? And the men slipped into her room to get their money's worth. Every day. Ten times a day.

Mama's face popped into her mind again. The ache spread.

No. She mustn't let the ache spread. Gabby pushed her mind back to her right toe.

Mama had worked so hard to take care of Gabby. Daddy died when Gabby was three years old, when Mama took her to Italy to live with Grandfather. Gabby liked spending hours with Mama and her grandpa at the dress shop, watching them work. Mama's hands were skilled, like Grandfather's, and she'd also begun teaching Gabby to sew.

But that was all gone now—Grandfather, dead. The shop was sold to pay his debts. And Mama. Mama was gone, too.

Gabby had no one.

Drip. Drip. Drip.

Gabby tried to think of something else. Perhaps the memory game Mama had taught her.

"You have to keep your brain muscle working," Mama had said. "To keep it strong, you must use it." Then she would give Gabby a long number to memorize and test her repeatedly. "Remember this number, Gabby; it could save your life."

What did that mean? Didn't matter. She still remembered the last ten digits of the number because that part was always the same. Mama switched the rest of the number around to try to throw Gabby off, but the last ten digits stayed constant. They were etched in Gabby's memory now.

But the memory game wasn't Gabby's favorite. Her favorite was the noticing game. They'd go for walks on the busy streets, and Mama would tell her to notice things—people's shoes, their hair color, their facial expressions. Then Mama would question Gabby about this person or that. That game was the most fun. Mama said Gabby should be observant, and Gabby was. She was good at the noticing game.

Drip. Drip. Drip.

Gabby stared at the ceiling. Seventeen cracks ran through it—four going sideways, thirteen long ways. She'd noticed. And she'd noticed the important customers by how the house mistress spoke to them just before she would open Gabby's door to let them inside. Her tone changed, and Gabby always noticed. Those men paid a lot more, she guessed.

But Gabby forgot her mother's words the last time she tried to escape. She should have realized her attempt to make it to the US Embassy would fail. She was stark naked. People noticed her. How could you miss a naked twelve-year-old running through the street? Her mother had always said to blend in. Don't draw attention. She had forgotten.

That's what she would do differently next time. Next time, she'd find a way to get some clothes before escaping.

Next time.

Drip. Drip. Drip.

What if she got caught next time, too? Last time, they'd beaten her so badly she peed bright-red blood for days. They'd even brought in a doctor to give her shots. They couldn't risk losing her. She brought in too much money for the house.

Gabby's toe throbbed. The water in the pipes dripped. Footsteps sounded on the stairs.

Gabby squeezed her eyes shut. Another man. She focused on her toe.

The headmistress's voice outside Gabby's door, speaking Turkish. "This way, sir."

Gabby opened her eyes and waited. Counted cracks on the ceiling. Pushed the needle under her toe. She listened to the pipes. She'd take it for now. But then she'd find another chance to escape. She'd get clothes so she would blend in. She'd make it to the US Embassy and leave this place behind—next time.

The needle jammed under her toenail, hot like fire.

Drip. Drip. Drip.

CHAPTER EIGHTEEN

David turned and looked at Jill. He watched as her foot tapped against the makeshift box while she sat on the square, lime-green sofa. It was the first hint to David of what was about to come. Jill's quirk was an endlessly tapping foot. She unwittingly did this when something was wrong, signaling David to get the hell out of the way. "What the heck is going on?" Jill demanded.

David stood in the doorway watching her, then turned. "I'll get us a drink. We have a lot to discuss." Jill did not reply. "Cab sav, okay?"

"I, uh, I don't feel like having anything to drink right now."

David walked into the room, hesitated, then walked to Jill, placed the glasses onto the makeshift coffee table, and poured a healthy amount of wine into each one. He handed Jill her glass and tipped his, clinking it into hers. "Cheers!"

"Cheers? Cheers! What the hell is there to be cheerful about?" she snapped before taking a large gulp of wine.

David stared at her as he sipped. She shot him a look of disdain as their faces played poker. They both knew that the first one who spoke would lose control of the conversation—control of the imminent argument that was about to unfold. David knew there was no way in hell she was giving up control now—no way in hell.

After several minutes of silence and sipping, David spoke first. "I know it's a bit of a mess." It was all he could get out before she interrupted.

"Who the hell is following me, David?" Jill demanded. "And why in the hell am I here, halfway around the world in Turkey of all places? Did you hear the news about the airport? What do you know about it? Why are you here? I want to know," Jill said sharply, then she stood fast, clunking the glass onto the trunk, almost breaking its stem. She marched across the room and turned. This move signaled David to hold on as the real reason for this argument was about to fly at him full force. "Why did you not let me know you were alive—that you were okay?" Then Jill's fingers quoted, and she gave a sing-song, "Hi Jill, it's David. I'm alive."

"Jill." David started to lift himself off the sofa.

But it was too late to get to the floor. "Do you even know what I went through? What I'm going through right now? Do you even give a crap?"

"I, uh ..."

Jill continued, spittle spraying in the air. "What was our marriage, David? Was it all for your case? All for the show?" David had only seen her angry like this once before, and he knew that any response would twist her even harder. The best thing he could do right now was to let her unwind before she twisted her head off or picked something up and threw it at him.

Jill turned and huffed, her arms crossed, and seconds passed before David spoke. "You done? Come on, sit down so we can talk rationally." As soon as he finished his sentence, he realized he should have waited longer to speak.

"Rationally!" Jill charged toward the glass of wine, picked it up, and took a swig. Red spittle flung through the air. "Rationally. I went into northern Afghanistan looking for you, David." She was vibrating now. She took another swig, emptied the glass, and plunked it down on the table. Jill's hand shook as she picked up the bottle and attempted to pour more wine, and for a split second, David thought Jill was about to take the bottle in both hands and chug down the wine directly from the bottle. It splashed into the glass as she poured it before she took another drink.

"You show up at the airport for only a minute. Clearly, you're alive. Then you tell me I must be careful, that someone may be following me. Then, poof, you're gone again." Jill made an exaggerated flick of her wrists, palms up in the air, almost spilling what was left in her glass.

"Then, imagine this ... I get to Turkey, and not only was the airport blown up at my scheduled landing time, but on my way to meet you... newsflash." Jill's fingers quoted. "I'm being followed. No, I'm being kidnapped by some big black dude pretending to be a taxi driver."

David stood fast and went to grab Jill. But Jill was faster. "Don't," she snapped as she lifted the glass of wine and held it high as if she were about to pitch a baseball toward David's head. This paused David.

They both stood silently, the stance freeze-framed, but only for a second before he smirked. "You gonna kill me with that? It'd be a shame to waste a 1989 cab sav."

David watched her face morph from a scowl to her poker face then to a smirk. He sat back down and poured himself another glass of wine and smiled at Jill. He knew he had won this round when she lowered her glass and sighed.

He hoped her rage was interrupted now, and he watched as she sank into the sofa. Jill looked forlorn as she stared at the floor.

David placed his glass down, reached down the side of his chair, and pulled a file from his case. "Okay, Jill." He paused then said, "You deserve to know what is happening; you deserve to know the truth."

CHAPTER NINETEEN

The room had no feeling of feng shui; if it wasn't for the furniture, it could pass as a large closet. David leaned forward, placed the file on the table, and sipped wine. "There's more wine."

Jill didn't say anything. All she could do was give a nod. She was more than frustrated. Right now, she was exhausted. All these weeks were steamrolling toward her all at once. And now David wanted to clue her in. She didn't know if she had the strength right now, really. She looked up at David as he flipped open the file and stopped. Jill's foot was tapping the table again.

"You want to just read this yourself?" he asked.

"Just tell me the truth, David," Jill snapped as she pulled her leg onto the sofa and tucked it under her butt cheek. David picked up the file and glass of wine and leaned back.

Closing the folder, he said, "Well, you know I'm a NOC for the OGA. I have been for almost three years. I was already on target when I met you. It was February when Paul recruited me; he's my case officer. I remember it was cold in the desert. It was a simple assignment for Time, a humanitarian story of U.S. doctors helping the poor. No armed action in the area. He introduced himself and asked if I would meet him in Kabul later that night. When we met there, he told me about a pending assignment. He wanted to recruit me to be part of the NOC program. I'd heard of such assignments; it's common in journalism. Given my role at Time, I asked him why. Long story short, he told me about Stan and disclosed that Stan was not my birth father and that I was adopted. At first, I thought, who is this crazy-ass guy sitting across from me? But it made sense. Then he showed me my adoption order from the court. I guess it didn't seem to be a shock. It was as if I knew already. Weird." David looked at her. She was just still, listening, and he continued. "The short story is, after several meetings, he offered me a job as a NOC. The money supplemented my income when I was between assignments. It was easy. He described the job as just relaying HUMINT, eh—"

"I know what human intelligence is, David," she said scornfully.

"Well, the more I learned about Stan, his history, his past, the more I began to despise him on a much deeper level for what he was attempting to do to our country. It wasn't for money, or at least I didn't think so then. It was for control. It was all about control for him," David trailed off.

"So, you knew ... you knew you were adopted before we met?" Jill questioned ruefully.

David sighed. "Yes." He shifted his puppy-dog look in Jill's direction. "I couldn't tell you, Jill. I couldn't say anything about Stan to you. I couldn't take the chance that he might notice something different. Learn the truth about me: I knew he wasn't my biological father." David paused, still in a deadlock stare. "It's why we never saw them."

"But ... but I thought that was because you didn't like them. Because they abused you. Because you thought they were evil," Jill said, puzzled. After all, this was the premise of David's family their whole marriage.

David broke the standoff, finished what was left in his glass, hesitated, and nodded. "That's all true, Jill. Everything I told you about them is true." David looked down. "After being put on target, I discovered things were much worse than Stan being a lousy father. It's why I didn't want him around us. Around you. I couldn't involve you, Jill. I just wouldn't."

Jill felt her face soften. "Why didn't you tell me where you were? All that time, I was looking for you. You must have known. Why didn't you try to reach..." Jill paused, her eyes narrowed, staring directly at David's. "The mate of your soul."

He slid over next to her. She looked away when he placed his forearm on her shoulder and began running his fingers through her hair, lightly scratching her scalp, and whispered, "What I do for our government, for our country, Jill, is not unlike what you do. Miss Psychic Queen."

Jill shrugged his hand off her shoulder. "Psychic Queen! Screw off, David. Don't change the subject. It's called deflection. It's an overused tactic where you push another issue onto me, making it my responsibility. Don't patronize me, David."

"I'm not, Jill," the pace of his voice quickened. "I ... I just find it fascinating that you were on my heels, pretty much my whole journey. Don't get me wrong; I wasn't aware of your tail until my caseworker told me in Hamburg." The right side of his mouth creased. "Of course, there was Zayed and also Leila." David's eyes narrowed slightly. "It's how you found me, right?"

Jill turned and studied his face. It was neither Leila nor Zayed that pointed her in the direction of Hamburg. In fact, it was David's notebook that she had found in that abandoned villa in Kushka that led her to Hamburg. Nothing else. No one else. But maybe she had been wrong about that. Was it strategically placed there for her to find it? She'd compartmentalize this fact for later. The mention of these two names made her pause before deciding what to say next. David knew Leila; they had worked together and were friends. She'd start there first. "Leila, what do you mean Leila?" Jill queried. "Have you talked to her?"

David leaned back into the sofa cushion and stared blankly at the coffee table box.

"What do you know about Leila?" David answered her question with a question. Jill saw it first before she felt it. It was the way he moved when he said her name. It was slight, but she thought she saw David sink further into the couch. Her sinking feeling coincided.

"You didn't answer me, David. Have you talked to Leila?"

He just shook his head blankly. "Zayed. It was Zayed who told you to go to Hamburg. Frankly, I think he was leading you on your little adventure to find me. Or to disclose to you what I was doing. You do know what he does for a living, right?"

Jill shot him a look. Again, changing the subject from Leila. She thought of Zayed.

"Zayed Saleem, your PRO officer? Or Zayed Mohammed." Jill tilted her head, sternly watching David's expression. A hint of recognition grew on David's face. "Yeah, I know I was his target for the CIA. A babysitter." Jill paused and waited. He said nothing. "Some babysitter ... a good-looking Arab. Really, David. What was that all about? Did you pick him yourself? Thought with his long hair and strong looks, he'd keep me preoccupied? Oh, and before you tell me more bullshit, I know he is an independent intelligence broker, David."

Jill's voice scratched through to the next sentence. "So, you do know Zayed? Do you know what happened to him?" The questions spilled out of Jill. "He was flown to Dubai, where Leila and I last saw him in the hospital."

Jill did see him after that in her last successful Remote Viewing session. But she wasn't going to disclose this to David now. Maybe not ever. In the RV, Jill viewed Zayed tortured and burned to death in the desert. She hadn't heard from him again.

David's demeanor darkened as if a shadow moved over his face. "He's dead."

"He was set on fire and burned to death." Jill's eyes lowered as she pushed out the words.

David flinched. "How did you know that?"

Jill sighed wearily. "I'm the Psychic Queen, remember?"

David's phone began to vibrate. Sighing, David snatched the phone from his shirt pocket and swiped it. "Hello?"

The voice on the phone bellowed, "Get out! Evac. Get out now."

The phone shut off; confusion grew on David's face, pushing the darkness away. With one swoop of his arm, the wine bottle and glasses crashed off the trunk, smashing onto the floor. He opened the clasp, lifted the lid, grabbed the Sig, and handed it to Jill. "Get ready," he commanded as he tucked a gun into the back of his waistband.

"What is..."

David stuffed the file into his backpack before slinging it over his shoulder.

"They're coming."

"Who's coming?"

David grabbed her arm and pulled her up. Then pulled the phone out of his pocket, swiped it, then tapped on the door unlock code. "The Gladios!" he yelled as they ran out the door.

CHAPTER TWENTY

She worked most nights, and it wasn't until the wee hours of the morning that they would let her rest—let her toe rest. She knew it was Sunday night because the brothel wasn't busy. It was the only night of the week that things were not as bad. People were busy getting ready for the start of a new week. She heard the other girls talking about it, and most men with families were active. She had waited two weeks now. She had counted the days. She had calculated that it would be a Sunday night when she tried to escape again. Even the pudgy woman was not hovering about.

Every night when everyone slept, Gabby would unlock her bedroom door. On her first escape attempt, she'd figured out that all the doors were locked with the same key. And it didn't take much thought to pinch the greasy guard's key when he rolled off her and snorted as he fell asleep.

She had to move fast. She slid slowly off the bed and hid the key. They had searched her room and even punched her in the stomach before pulling her hair and pushing her to the floor. It was worth it. She knew they would never again punch her in the face, as they didn't want to sell damaged goods. Besides, she was still recovering from her "sickness," so they were lenient with her. The other girls weren't so lucky.

Every night since she'd unlocked the door, she sometimes waited up to two hours. She waited and listened. Sometimes, she would hear sounds on the cement floors in the evening, like thuds from something heavy. But the sounds never revealed anything of danger to her. There was no threatening waft of alcohol breath huffing in her face or on her back. She would sometimes hear the sound of one of the girls having a nightmare. How could they not after what they had to endure? She had planned it. She had rehearsed it over and over and over. They didn't give any of the girls footwear. It was a precaution, she thought. She'd have to go barefoot again. But this time, she figured out how to wrap the stained bed sheet around her frail body and make it look almost like a dress. It wasn't much, but it was better than being naked.

Today was Sunday. Today was the night, all right. Tonight was the night.

CHAPTER
TWENTY-ONE

The dark street illuminated the headlights of the black SUV that halted directly in front of the safe house door. "Get in!" David shouted.

Jill slid into the back seat; he slid in behind her before the driver jammed his foot on the gas. "Hold on."

"How did they find us? How did they know?" barked David.

"We got the call minutes ago. We didn't have time to vet it. But we suspect it was from one of our HUMINTs. They couldn't confirm the sender," replied Allan, who was maneuvering the SUV off the cobblestone and onto the main road.

"Allan Mars, this is Jill Oliver. She's working with us on a special assignment."

Allan looked at Jill in the rearview mirror and nodded before taking a hard right. David held Jill as they took the turn.

David said, "It's okay to talk in front of Allan, Jill. He's a spook like me. He's been working on the Operation Gladio project."

"I heard you were coming," Allan said bluntly. "You're causing quite a stir now, Miss Oliver."

"What, me? I ... uh. Special assignment for who?" she stammered, gave David a one-eyed stare, and continued her query.

David returned the folder to his bag and handed it to Jill. "It's all in there. It's what I was starting to explain."

Jill flipped open the file and began to read. Her response was quick. "Wait a minute. My assignment for Europol is what, fake?"

"Not exactly. We had to vet your cover story, so I guess I'd say, sort of," said David.

"So, what is my assignment exactly? It says here you need to recruit me. Recruit me for what?" Jill caught a glance from Allan and then looked over at David.

"Well, tomorrow, you were set to meet with Moneyval. Your assignment with Europol—it's to do with Moneyval." Jill gave him a poker face; this new information about her assignment pissed her off. She hated being left in the dark. Hated it. "Moneyval is ... well ... a group of experts that research and evaluate any anti-money-laundering measures for financing terrorism. They're the monitoring body for the Council of Europe, aka Europol."

Another glance from Allan, and Jill noted this. David continued, "There is a keen interest in what the Moneyval people will uncover."

"Uncover?" David paused. "There are indications that some of the financings for the Gladios and Gladio operations came from... came from US sources."

"Sources, what sources?" questioned Jill. "Are you saying our government has been funding terrorism?" This statement vibrated through Jill's soul. It was her job as a US Marshal and terrorist profiler to stop such groups—such people. But were they funding terrorism in Turkey? It made no sense.

"Why would the US fund terrorism?" she asked. But before he could answer her question, she kept talking. "And why in Turkey? I mean... I know about such black ops and their strategies to protect the US. But what does Turkey have to do with protecting the US?"

"Well, it's only a theory at this point, but the chatter gives us indicators that ISIS is involved."

This word stopped Jill from continuing her inquisition, and she thought about what David had just said. The only sound you could hear was the thrum of the SUV's engine. Nobody spoke for several minutes, and then David said, "Right now, we have reliable indicators but nothing concrete. Moneyval will not disclose its findings for another week. It's why you are here, Jill. We need a mole. We need to know what they know now. We have other assets on target, but we need someone on the inside."

Jill looked directly into David's eyes. "A mole? You mean a spy?"

David said nothing.

"I'm not a spy, David. I'm a crime analyst and a researcher. How do you suppose I will be able to spy on Moneyval? Just walk in, grab some papers on someone's desk, and walk out?" Jill crossed her arms. "Besides, can't the CIA just ask them?" A thought struck her hard as she began grasping what was happening. "Okay, so the CIA wants a heads-up on their findings as to 'who.'" Jill's fingers quoted the air. "Who is funding these Gladios?"

"Well, yes and no," David replied.

"The Gladios?" Jill said pointedly. "Who are these Gladios? You said they are the ones chasing us. Is that who is following us?"

David looked at her, then back at the road. "I'm not sure exactly."

Jill crossed her arms and waited. Her body was tossed around as the SUV merged onto the main highway.

David leaned back and hesitated before he said, "The Gladios have been in Turkey for many years. They are now considered to be a terrorist group. They're like a secret stay-behind NATO army from a very long time ago and are now connected with the mafia, the Chechen mafia, to be exact. But they're protected by the government and others—" David didn't finish his sentence as Jill interrupted.

"Mafia?"

"Well, it's more than just a mafia, Jill. The Gladios are different. They're paramilitary."

Allan cleared his throat. "The Gladios, or more importantly, Operation Gladio, was the codename for a clandestine NATO stay-behind operation in Europe in the '50s. The purpose was to provide armed resistance against a Soviet invasion. With this end-game as the operation's target, they created super-secret armies in at least fourteen European countries—today coined Operation Gladio B."

Jill felt like she was in a scene from a spy novel, but she continued to listen.

"But the stay-behind army stayed behind longer than reported and still operates today," Allan said.

David added, "But now the group has evolved—I guess you can say. They are connected to many black ops groups, including the Chechen guerrillas they consider their brothers."

Allan continued, "Since the mid-1990s, the Gladio Bs have been an untold instrument for governments to manipulate and control the democracies of Western Europe from within. Their strategy has led to terror and fear in the general populations of countries where they operate." Allan paused for a beat and continued, "They're unknown to lower layers of government and mainstream media. They participate in ruthless terrorist attacks against their people to instill fear, control the population, and frame left-wing political opponents."

"What the hell," Jill blurted. "Why are they after you, and why me?"

David sat in silence. Jill watched as his face showed a ruminating stare.

"I know you probably don't know what I was doing in Afghanistan. My mission in Afghanistan—why I was there? Why was Stan Brown my target?"

"No, they said it was classified; even Leila couldn't find anything. Or so she said." Jill gave him a sideways look. "Other than it had something to do with the Chechen mafia. Wait. Do you think it was the Gladios in Afghanistan? Operation Gladio B? I heard about Operation Silhouette."

Allan glanced back; his body bobbled from side to side as he jolted in and out of lanes. Jill thought about the men who were following her in Tucson. Eric thought they were rogue Chechens, a disbanded group from the main Chechen mafia, and then she thought about Doha and Kushka.

Jill turned to David. "Is this the same Chechen mafia trailing Zayed and me when we were trying to find you?"

Allan glanced back at David, then flicked his vision back to the road. "What do you mean?" David asked.

Jill thought about what to say as she looked at Allan and then back to David. "When I was first in Doha, eh ... with Zayed. They were after me. Or that's what Zayed had told me. He said it was the Chechen mafia in Doha. It's a long story, but they followed us the whole trip. And even before I left for Tucson, I felt like someone was following me. Later, Eric—you know my old boss," Jill added for Allan. "He told me, based on intel, he thought it was a group of men who had broken off from the main Chechen mafia—they were in Tucson just before I left for Doha."

David's eyes bulged slightly at this disclosure. "I did not know about your trip other than what my case officer told me. Maybe he didn't know. It's the first I've heard of this intel. Maybe something is connecting them." David stared at the back of the driver's seat.

"There's more, Jill. It's deep-rooted, and the more we dig, the more we discover, the more we don't know. See, Stan was my target because of the Grozny pipeline in Chechnya. Stan's company was neck-deep in planning the pipeline when it was first designed. This pipeline is critical."

Jill remembered what Zayed had said about Grozny, and she thought about the schematic she found with David's notebook in Kushka. She still had it in her bag.

"I know about the Grozny pipeline. Zayed told us. Well, Leila and I. It's currently under the control of the Chechens, right?"

David nodded. "I can see why the Russians want control back. That's the Stan Brown connection. He's part of a larger group, but I believe this goes far beyond the usual government channels—beyond handshakes behind closed doors."

"So, let me get this straight. Do you mean a group of men from all those different countries are working together? How is that even possible? I mean, there is no love between Russia and Chechnya. Why would they be allies?"

"It's deeper than just superficial geopolitical squabbles, Jill. It's bigger than that. There's a silent war with secret armies vying for control of more than just Russian oil."

"Control of what?" Jill pushed.

"World power," David said, staring at the back of the seat before him and not connecting with Jill's glance.

"World power?" Jill thought about it. She envisioned a group of men standing in black cloaks surrounding and chanting around a carving of a star on a wooden floor—the Star of David. "You mean like a new world order?" She considered telling David about her viewing, about Leila's research in Brussels, about the fire that burned the Star of David from the old wooden floor in the basement of the church there. But right now, she didn't trust him. Right now, she didn't trust anyone. And right now, she didn't even trust herself.

"What does this have to do with Turkey? And me? I mean, do they know I'm set to go into Moneyval tomorrow? Is that what this is all about?"

"Have you ever heard about the self-named Afghan Mujahideen Freedom Fighters and how the CIA supplied the Stinger missiles that defeated the Soviet army occupying Afghanistan for ten years?"

"It's common knowledge now, yes. But again, what does this have to do with me?"

Allan looked back again. Jill noticed the glance he held with David was longer than it should have been. She looked at David. There was something in the way David moved. Did she really see it? It was ever so slight, but Jill knew it was there. She knew. Jill had studied many faces as a profiler. Jill didn't hate much, but she did hate liars. There it was again, that body language when he captured Allan's eyes once more. It was so subtle that the average person would not have noticed it—recognized it. But Jill did, and then a thought kicked at her heart. She slowly moved her hand down the right side of her pant leg and felt her gun. She had put the safety on when she got into the SUV. A dumb move, she thought now. Why hadn't she, over the past year, seen anything suspicious about David? Why was she just noticing this now? Were all these signs here all this time? They must have been. Then why hadn't she recognized them? Maybe she was too caught up. After all, why would she even think something was wrong? David was attentive, loving, and sexy as hell in bed. Maybe she didn't want to know, or maybe, just maybe, she didn't care. Maybe she just wanted him.

No one was talking now, and Jill leaned back and absorbed her thoughts. That nagging thought was still poking at her—the thought that something was not quite right. Jill sighed again. Maybe she was just paranoid. You know that old saying: Just because I'm paranoid doesn't mean they're not after me. But she had learned how to be aware of her paranoia indicators and knew what would happen If she didn't squash the PTSD beast, and with that thought, she asked, "Tell me more about the Gladios... and the Chechens." She closed her eyes. The vehicle slowed and took a hard right. Jill sat up fast, looked ahead, and noticed they were no longer on the main highway. "Where are we going?"

"Later, I can get you a brief on them when we go in," David said, not looking at Jill.

"Go in?" Jill's head tilted slightly. "Go in where?"

"We're going to HQ; it's connected to the American Embassy. It's not a five-star hotel or anything, but we'll be safe there until the brief in the morning. Hell, I'd be surprised if the team hasn't already been summoned."

"Team?" Jill queried.

Allan peered into the rearview mirror before flicking his eyes back ahead. David leaned slightly forward, pulling the phone from his pocket. "It's almost two a.m." They rode in silence for several more minutes.

Jill looked at him and demanded, "Who is this team, David?"

"Okay, okay," he stammered. "The team is, well... the brass, you might call them, not the grassroots, undercover folks like us. High-level stuff here on the ground."

"So, these are the people from Europol we are meeting?"

"No. CIA brass."

Jill felt like she was playing a game of Clue. "You're not answering my question. What do these Gladios want with us, David?"

David looked forward as if mulling over what to say next. Ignoring her first question and answering her second one, he said, "I've been trying to extrapolate that, Jill."

Allan's eyes flickered with recognition in the rearview.

"At this point, I can't figure that out. One thing I can tell you, though, is that if they want us, we'd be dead by now."

Jill watched David as he subtly checked his nine o'clock. Then over Jill's lap to his three o'clock, and he continued. "So, as far as I can tell, they want us alive."

"Alive? Why? I didn't even know what a Gladio was until now."

David nodded. "That's why it's perplexing." David looked towards Allan. His stare deepened, intensifying as if the answer was knocking on his mind's door, with recognition fueling his gaze. David tensed his hand, which had already begun forming a fist. Jill shoved her hand hard into her side pocket. She was too late. It was the last thing Jill saw coming.

CHAPTER TWENTY-TWO

The villa was quiet now; her room was dark. She could hear no sounds echoing through the cement walls. No sounds. Nothing. Gabby began to wrap the bed sheet around her as if making a toga dress. She wrapped one corner of the sheet around once, took each of the other corners over one shoulder, and tied them together. She pulled the pillowcase off the grungy pillow, twisted it, and tied the makeshift belt around her waist. She lifted the leg of the old metal bed frame, and a small golden key tinkled onto the concrete floor. She picked it up and rubbed it while deep in thought. The bed sheet was dark enough, almost a faded brown color. It would help her blend into the night. It was the one mistake she made on her last attempt. This time, she was more determined than ever. She would make it inside the Embassy. She knew in her heart and now in her brain. She knew she would make it.

But she had to ensure no one would hear her. If someone did, they'd know where she was going. One of the regular men who had visited her told her exactly where the Embassy was. "It's not far from this brothel, but please do not leave here," he'd slur as she gave him his delight. He was drunk enough to let her know, she thought at the time. But she learned quickly nothing was ever for free. She paid the price. It hadn't hurt that bad. She had thought of her toe—the searing pain in her toe. And she knew. She knew more than anything; she'd do it again. She knew she would.

Gabby moved toward the door, leaned her face against its crack between the jamb, and listened. She counted in her head. She'd done this many times since they recaptured her. She counted at all different times of the night. She already knew that at one a.m., the last patron would be leaving. They would finish cleaning the rooms before Madam grabbed a bottle of something and retreated to her room, locking the door behind her.

Then there were the last two men. The guards. Sometimes they would open one of the other girls' doors, and sometimes they'd come into Gabby's room. The grunting would continue for only a few minutes. Gabby cringed at the memories and thought of her toe.

But it was Sunday night; they'd already had their fill for this week, or so she'd hoped. It was always Sunday when they would sit and drink, counting their pay. It was Sunday when they'd watched TV and appeared to have let their guard duties slide. It was Sunday Gabby had tested twice and proved to herself it was the right night of the week to attempt another escape.

Time passed with more counting. Gabby heard nothing. She slowly inserted the key, leaned her left arm against the door, pushed it, and gently twisted the deadbolt.

There was no sound, just the waft of cigarette smoke that lingered in the air. She stepped through the doorway, turned, and softly closed the door behind her. She inserted the key again, lightly pulling on the knob, and slowly locked the door.

Suddenly, Gabby froze and held her breath. Only the shudder of her heartbeat filled her ears. She waited for a beat. "Tick. Tick. Tick." She paused and turned to look into the dim, ambient light coming from under one of the doors. There was also a different smell in the air—one she hadn't smelled before. Something like a burnt match. Like fire. "Tick. Tick. Tick." Gabby looked up, trying to understand what was happening. "Tick. Tick. Tick." She saw it. The air vent above the door was blowing warm scented air and was making a strange sound as if the motor was winding up too fast. It was a broken exhaust fan, she thought. She remembered her grandfather's home on the hot summer nights. The kitchen smell would float through the house, expelling the aromas from the evening dinner. Someone was cooking. It was "her," she thought, and then breathed a slight sigh, blowing out her breath.

She began to pussyfoot through the dark hallway to the top of the marble-clad stairway. She stopped at the top, spied down the dark stairs, and listened. She knew how many stairs there were and began to descend. Two steps. Listen. Two steps. Listen. Two steps. Listen. She did that six more times, going down the winding stairwell.

At the bottom was a long hallway. Light from the living room bounced off its cement walls. She could hear a cacophony of grumbles, rhythmic by nature, and then a snort. Those bastards were sleeping. Hope pinched her, and she continued to move.

She slowly approached the archway that was the entrance to the kitchen, turned, and pressed her back to the cold wall, and listened. The sound of sleep see-sawed, filling the room. She could do this again. She knew she could. Just go. Just go. Just go.

The only way she knew she could get out of the villa was through the kitchen, into an outdoor kitchen, then through the courtyard. It was a small yard, and an enclosed cubby shed in one corner held the garbage. Her plan was simple. Open the garbage storage doors from the patio, then move the trash. Step in, open the doors from where the garbage was collected on the street side of the ten-foot concrete fence, then close the courtside doors. She'd rehearsed it over and over. No one would know she was gone until the first client came in the morning. It was a good plan. A solid plan, she hoped.

Walking through the kitchen was easy. The back door to the outdoor kitchen would be locked. But she knew where the key was. Because the outdoor kitchen was hardly ever used, they kept one sitting on top of the door's thick molding for when they took out the garbage. Gabby slowly slid open the cupboard drawer and found the tongs she had placed aside. She slowly lifted them out, pulled on the end, released the clip, opening the claws. Gabby moved over to the locked door, stood on the balls of her feet, reached up with the tongs, and attempted to pinch the key from the ledge. She held her breath. If she missed, the key would clang to the floor. The dull night light from the wall socket glowed as she tried to clip the key and missed. She stood back down and stared at the key, almost willing it to jump into her hand.

What was that? Gabby turned when she heard a sound. She sucked in a breath and listened. Someone was stirring in the room where the two men slept. She didn't have much time. She knew. She knew. She knew. Gabby turned back to the door and tried to grab the key again. The tongs clinked as they clipped the key. She maneuvered the key into the palm of her hand, placed the tongs gently onto the granite countertop, stuck in the key, and twisted the lock open. She slid through the door and closed it. She didn't have time to fumble and lock the door again in the dark.

Clouds blocked the moon as she left the dark outdoor kitchen, stepped down, and entered the courtyard. A large water pump connected to an oversized white plastic tank occupied most of the space. The lack of noise from the water pump told Gabby that no one was running water in the villa. No showers or flushing toilets. Silence.

Gabby darted towards the thick cement wall surrounding the villa and approached the garbage bin doors. A giant gecko scurried along the wall in front of her before disappearing into a crack. Gabby cringed at the thought of what might be in the dark garbage cubby. But she didn't care about rats right now, or anything else for that matter. She reached the metal doors and pulled down on the lever hard. It released its grip on the wall jamb. The sound of metal scraping metal ground into the night as she pulled the doors open. The putrid smell slapped her in the face. She gasped when several rats scurried over her bare feet. Inside were bags of hot garbage. The hum of insects surrounded them. It was dark inside, but Gabby stepped forward, her mind struggling between hesitation and determination. A trash bag cracked as she stepped on it. It was pitch black as she continued to step forward. Her hands held straight before her, she reached for the opposite door and its handle. Finding it, she pulled the lever down, simultaneously pushing on the door that opened onto the street. It wouldn't budge. Was it locked? Did the sanitation workers use a key? Gabby squeezed out a whimper.

Suddenly, lights flicked on in the villa, illuminating a third-floor window. Startled, Gabby pushed and pulled. Pushed and pulled. She tripped over the piles of bags as the doors swung open. Her palms scraped across the gravel as she fell out onto the ground.

CHAPTER
TWENTY-THREE

Jill screamed as the truck twisted and sped down the road. Allan's body slumped over the steering wheel. It only took a rabbit punch from David, a quick, sharp strike to the back of the head—well, three actually—to knock Allan out. David scrambled over the seat, squished Allan's limp body to the right over the console, and attempted to regain control of the SUV.

Everything happened at the same time. "What the hell are you doing?" Jill shrieked.

David grunted. The truck fishtailed sideways. He cranked the wheel hard and straightened its course. He kicked Allan's foot off the gas pedal and slammed on the brake. Jill's body lurched forward as dust from the sandy road puffed around the SUV when it came to a complete stop.

"Get out," David yelled. Jill grabbed the door handle and pulled. Nothing happened.

"I can't; it won't open," Jill retorted.

David jumped out and yanked the door open. Jill fell forward, spilling out of the truck. He caught her before she hit the ground. His arms hugged her as she steadied. "What the hell are you doing, David?"

Jill huffed as she pushed David's grip off her, stepped back, and fell into a fighting stance. She studied him quickly and pulled out her Sig.

David held up both hands, palms facing her. "Hold on, Jill!" He was breathing heavily. "Look, Jill, I had to do that. Look around," he said, jittery.

It was evident to Jill he was jacked up on adrenaline. Jill stood at the ready, staring directly at David. He turned and pointed his thumb behind his head. "See over there? Those are the lights of the American Embassy, down there by the river on that hill." Jill's eyes flicked over David's right shoulder, then back at him. "Allan was taking us away from the Embassy." David stared at Jill, huffed, and waited. "Look, Jill, I'm not going to hurt you." His palms were still up in the air facing her. "But Allan sure as hell was." He nodded toward the slumped figure in the SUV. "He's one of them."

Jill looked over at Allan, who wasn't moving. "What are you talking about? You said I could trust him. You vetted him, and now you just punched the shit out of him. Why would you do that? What the hell is going on now, David?" Jill demanded.

"I can explain, but we have to go."

"Go where? How?"

"We can't go in that vehicle. It's tracked. All agency vehicles are. But I'm afraid this one may also be under surveillance by them."

"Them?"

"The Gladios."

David reached for Jill's elbow. "Come on! I think it's only about five miles to the main road. We can find transportation, a taxi, or something."

"But..." Jill huffed, striding at David's speed. "What about Allan?"

David hastened his pace. "We won't have to worry about him. He's dead."

CHAPTER
TWENTY-FOUR

Matthew McGregor giggled, pulling back the skin of his hangnail, then tore it off. A tiny bead of blood bubbled before he licked it.

Matthew sat in the dark cell, Indian-style, his legs crossed, facing the steel bars, and spoke to no one. In a hushed voice, he whispered, "I know."

He giggled again. "They're stupid. How do they not know?" Another giggle. "Morons!"

Silence.

"Ah ha, yup. Ah ha, yup," Matthew yipped. "I saw her. She won't get away. She needs my help. I know. I know. I know." And he giggled again. "All these years. All these years, I've figured it out. I've figured out how to find you. How to see you."

Matthew began to rock and rock and rock. His voice began to deepen. "It was Mother who brought you to me—Mother who showed you the way. Mother did. Mother did. Mother? Stop yelling at me. I know." More rocking back and forth. Beads of sweat began to form on his upper lip as he rocked and rocked and rocked.

Suddenly, Matthew stiffened. "No. No. No." The chains rattled as he hit the sides of his head. Then, without hesitation, Matthew slumped forward and whimpered.

"Don't hurt me," he cried aloud. "I'll be good. I'll be good. I'm not a bad boy."

CHAPTER
TWENTY-FIVE

Pain rushed to Gabby's scraped knees. She hesitated for only a split second. It was her first thought. Her only thought, really. Gabby scrambled to her feet and ran. Run anywhere, run. Run now. She darted across the back street and into the maze of alleys, courtyards, and streets. Everything looked different than the first time she had tried to get into the embassy.

She felt the familiar tearing on the bottom of her feet that had just healed. Gravel ripped at the newly formed skin. She entered the sleeping alleyway and slowed to a stop. On the corner was a familiar shop. She'd seen it before. Steel rolling shutters covered its windows. And she remembered the sign. It was a picture of a dancing donkey. This way, she knew. This way. Adrenaline pushed her into the same alley she had gone to before the last time she tried to escape. Numbed pressure pushed at her feet each time her foot smacked the crunchy ground.

She ran through the end of the alley, ducked into a closed shop doorway, and peered around the concrete wall. It was there. She could see the American embassy. The street to its mammoth gate appeared empty. She shivered as she stood in the shadows, watching the entranceway of the embassy for what seemed like hours. She breathed and contemplated. There was no van—in fact, there was no movement. With resolve, she left her hiding space slowly, then fast and faster. She was breathing hard as she ran toward the embassy guardhouse. She heard something when she was only ten feet away from the entrance. A scream, or was it a shout? She kept her eye on the prize and pushed faster. And before she could stop herself, before she could figure out who was screaming, and before she recognized the sound of her voice, she ducked under the arm gate and began frantically banging on the guardhouse door.

CHAPTER
TWENTY-SIX

David stirred the coffee sludge in the white Styrofoam cup and handed it to Jill. The room looked like an executive airport lounge. Four large black leather couches surrounded a white laminate table.

"Thanks," Jill whispered, blowing on the coffee before setting it down.

"That was quite a run. A little hard in those boots." David looked at Jill's police-style black boots. "How are your feet? Glad we managed to flag that taxi, or we would still be out there," he said, avoiding the elephant in the room. He was troubled thinking about Allan. It's why they hadn't spoken during the impromptu PT—physical training. Allan. It wasn't the first time David had killed someone, and he knew exactly how to do it. He had known Allan from his Stan Brown assignment. Allan was an analyst, David's go-to guy for intel. He was harmless, really. Allan wasn't a field agent and wasn't a physical threat. And where was he taking them, anyway? David knew he didn't have to kill him, and if he hadn't, then maybe he could have gotten those questions answered. So why did he? David already knew.

David looked at Jill's untouched cup. "It's a little stale, but what can we ask for at this time of night?"

"So, no one is here yet?"

"No, I thought they would be here by now. I'm sure they're on their way."

"Maybe Allan just made it up that a meeting was being assembled. Where was he taking us, David? What do you know about him?"

"I wondered about the meeting, too, but I've had a confirmation text message." David pulled his thoughts together, sat down, placed the cup on the table, and leaned back. "You look revived. Guess a three-mile run kicked up your endorphins, huh?" David said as he watched Jill.

He wondered what she thought about Allan—about him. And before his mind could move down that path, Jill asked, "So why did you attack Allan? Why kill him? I thought you could trust him. And if you wanted to kill him, why not use your gun?" Jill questioned as she took a sip of the warm brew.

David studied her for a beat. "When I was at the restaurant waiting for you, I received a message from Paul—you know, my case officer. Anyway, they had discovered a mole filtering intel to Stan's group. They had it narrowed down to two operatives, but he couldn't say who over SMS, obviously. He was going to brief me when we had a secure line. He told me to watch my back. I had been thinking about who it could be, who had access to the intel about the Gladios. It wasn't until we were in the truck that I noticed Allan was not acting like himself. Usually, you can't shut him up, always chirping a dry joke that only he would laugh at. As we continued to travel, I studied him. Then I noticed he was going in the wrong direction. Honestly, I didn't think he would be such a pawn. But it seems to be happening all the time these days. Money is money, I guess."

"Gee, David, you've got some great colleagues," Jill sniped.

David ignored the jab and continued. "He seemed overly interested in you and our discussion. I guess that's normal for most people. But driving in a different direction, I... I don't know. It was pure instinct, I guess. I didn't mean to kill him. It was an accident."

"Accident? You punched him hard at the base of his skull. Anyone who has ever taken a basic self-defense course knows that a rabbit punch is, in most cases, lethal. Never mind that it's against the law to use. And for a good reason: it can cause serious and irreparable spinal cord injury or detach the brain from the brain stem. That's probably what killed him; probably killed him instantly, I might add." Jill took another sip.

David looked down at his feet. He knew Jill was watching him. "I've heard of this type of double cross before, just never experienced it myself." His head lifted, and he raised his cup as if to say cheers but instead said solemnly, "All in a day's work in the spy business." And he took a sip of his coffee.

"Who was he a mole for, David? Who is the enemy here?"

"I got to thinking while we were jogging. It can't be the Gladios. It's gotta be someone other than the Gladios."

"Why? Right, we'd be dead by now if it was them. The Chechens, then?"

David gave a slight shrug as he contemplated.

"We need to find out," Jill said. "Otherwise, I'm not leaving this building. Do you think this has to do with this Moneyval meeting? I mean, am I still going to sail in there..." Jill looked around the room. "The day has already started, and I am not even close to being prepared for anything now." David followed Jill's scan. White mini blinds covered four panes of glass. No light was coming through yet, but the clock on the wall read 5:54 a.m.

David gave a hollow nod. "We're able to stay in here until the meeting. If you want to microwave something from the fridge, there's a kitchenette." David pointed in the direction of the refrigerator. "There are also showers complete with jail cell towels. As I said, it's no five-star hotel or anything. But a shower sounds good about now."

"Where are the showers?"

"Down the corridor to the left. Keep going straight past the holding area. You can't miss it. I will give the Commander another call and get an ETA."

"Commander?"

"I call him Commander because it's easier than his full title: Deputy Director of Intelligence and Foreign Affairs for this region. And I need to contact Paul about Allan. I will need to brief him in writing, but I can at least confirm we're here. Go ahead and grab a shower. Ladies first."

CHAPTER
TWENTY-SEVEN

Jill had studied David as he gave an unreasonable answer to a reasonable question. She thought about what he had just said as she rifled through her bag. How could he not know a blow to the skull like that would kill Allan? There was no way he could not understand this if he was trained in CIA PT. They would have taught him this; it's in basic training. She needed time to think. She needed some time alone.

The adrenaline rush was wearing off. Jill reached for her bag and then walked out the door and down the hall in the direction David had gestured. Jill thought of waiting outside the door and listening to his conversation. But the door was heavy, probably soundproof, and she was tired. Jill needed the shower to wake her up. She needed the shower to help sort out her thoughts. But right now, she just didn't care. Maybe it was the jet lag. Or perhaps it was the fact that some Gladio mafia guys were trying to capture her. For what? She still did not know, but she sure as hell would find out at the meeting. She'd command the commander; that much she knew.

Jill moved in the direction David had told her. As she approached the holding area, she heard an unexpected sound. It sounded like a child whimpering. She entered the holding area and saw where the sound was coming from. A child sat on a black leather couch. Her arms were wrapped around her legs, and she hugged her knees tight. A baby-blue blanket was wrapped around her, and she was whimpering. Two women were directly across from where the child was sitting in the opposite corner of the room. One held up papers and pointed to the girl, whispering.

Jill looked back at the girl. The blanket covered most of her head and body. Strands of wet, greasy brown hair stuck out in disarray. Jill thought about what she should say. She should at least ask if everything was okay. The child's eyes pleaded something unspoken to Jill. "Are you alright?" Jill asked.

"Please," one of the women said. "Please do not upset the girl." Jill looked back at the two women, and the no-nonsense glare from one of them told Jill to mind her business.

Jill's gut twinged. She smiled in the child's direction and watched as a little tear bubble plopped on the girl's cheek as she blinked. Jill frowned, but she continued her quest for a shower.

Jill walked into the opposite corridor. Obviously, something was wrong with the girl. But what did Jill know about kids? It was strange for a girl that age to be in the American Embassy at this time of night. Clearly, neither of the two women whispering was her mother. They seemed too stiff and cold, and they sure as heck weren't comforting the poor girl. Something niggled at Jill. It was a feeling she couldn't wash off in the semi-warm shower. She'd approach the women and ask them more about the child when she got out. Sure, it was none of her business, but when did that ever stop her? When she walked back through the holding area, it was empty. The young girl and the two women were gone. Why was this troubling her? She'd ask David or whoever was in the meeting.

The lounge where she had last seen David was empty too. There was no sign of him. Jill placed her bag on the edge of the couch arm, claiming it for a pillow before sinking hard into the seat. And before she could bring herself into the tunnels—her intuitive tunnels to help organize her thoughts—she closed her eyes; darkness dropped like a theater curtain as she fell asleep.

It was hard to breathe. The air was stale, and if it weren't for the fan's hum, she wouldn't be able to breathe. It was dark as she tried to see. She tried to turn. She tried to lift her body. When she raised her hands to feel where she was, a sliver pricked the tip of one of her fingers. She sucked in a quick breath, almost whistling. She was more frightened than she had ever been. She tried to shake off the fog that filled her head. She'd been drugged before but had never felt so out of it. She was drifting in and out of consciousness, and all she wanted to do was sleep.

Blackness. Sleep. Blackness. Sleep. Then she heard a sound. What was it? A moan. She lay still, holding her breath, and listened. The sound came again, but a loud hum muffled it. She tried to feel around again, this time going slower. First, she moved her arms simultaneously on both sides of her body. The back of her hands scraped the sides within inches of herself. She turned her palms out and gently felt the rough wooden walls. She tapped her fingers as they spidered the walls before hitting the roof, just inches above her head. Where was she? A coffin? Then with recognition, she screamed. She punched her fists against the metal bars that grated the open space above her head. She suddenly stopped when she heard it again. Moaning. It was the sound of moaning. She waited and listened. She heard it again, but this cry sounded different, like it was coming from another direction.

Suddenly the box jolted. Then shaking. A bounce. More shaking. A flash of light illuminated the inside of her box. The glow began to strengthen. She tilted her head back and looked above it as she arched her back. Through the grate, she could see what looked to be a mirror. An image began to focus. The image in the mirror was a girl—the girl in the holding room.

"Jill! Jill!" Jill pawed the air, and David took a step back and watched. Jill became aware of her surroundings. She realized she had been dreaming and looked blankly in David's direction, trying to catch her breath. She stood and accidentally knocked her bag onto the floor.

She was breathing fast. "The girl," Jill shouted frantically.

"What girl?" David said, a perplexed look growing on his face.

"Eh..." Jill thought about her dream, then thought about her encounter earlier and blurted out, "There was a girl in the holding room. I saw her earlier. I just had a dream about her." Jill turned and hurried out the door and down the corridor to the holding area, with David fast behind her.

The waiting area was empty, precisely as Jill had last seen it. "There was a girl here?" David asked. "I didn't see a girl, Jill. What are you talking about?"

"She was sitting right here, David. And two women were standing over there, watching her and whispering."

"Whispering?"

"I couldn't hear what they were saying. But something was wrong with the girl. And now I just had a dream about her."

David just stared at her, then reached his arms, resting them on her shoulders. "Is this one of your dreams, Jill? You know, the ones you have now and then?"

Jill shot him a look, and for an instant, she felt she was in a void between her life with David and without him. For the most part, her PTSD was under control. She still did have the occasional nightmare. Why now? She had kept them at bay for at least a year—her year with David. They were stuffed in a locker somewhere deep in her mind. She had beaten the beast, beaten the demons that would not let her rest. As she stood before David, images of Matthew McGregor began to hit her out of the blue—another image of her mother. A little girl was hiding under the stairs. A little girl in a suitcase. A little... the images were spinning now. Spinning. Spinning. Spinning.

Jill began to feel light-headed, the warning signs of an impending panic attack. She sat down slowly. Was it a dream about this girl? Or was it the lingering nightmare of where her mother would keep her? She remembered what Dr. Erin Wildeman had told her. "There's an additional report about the condition of the house they found you in that day when you were little. The house would have been condemned if any health inspector had been allowed in. But they found something very disturbing in the main bedroom. Apparently, where your mother and male visitors would sleep, they found something under the bed. It was a large black cloth suitcase. Inside was a blanket soiled with urine and feces. Your mother confessed that this was where you slept when you were bad, very, very bad."

She sat staring at the spot where the young girl sat and began her yoga-style breathing.

"Jill," David cooed, interrupting her thoughts. "You okay?"

Jill didn't move—didn't speak. She just breathed. The first level, second level, third level. Hold and out. The first level, second level, third level. Hold and out. The first level, second level, third level. Hold and out. After several more breaths, Jill sighed. "I, ah, I don't... I guess so. It's just..." Jill's thoughts jumbled around. She considered telling

David about her dream. About the girl in the box. But what would he care? "I guess I'm just tired, jet lag, I suppose. But, I mean, is there any way you can find out who that young girl was? I, ah, I just want to know what happened to her, that's all."

Jill looked up and noticed a CCTV camera in the corner of the room. Determined, Jill stood and walked under it and turned towards David. She watched him look directly at the camera and then at his watch. "Look, Jill, they're almost assembled now for the meeting. We have to go. We can talk about this girl later. I'm sure she is fine."

Jill stormed past him, shoving him with her shoulder as she went by.

CHAPTER
TWENTY-EIGHT

The room's fluorescent lights were blinding as the man who had introduced himself as Ian Waters, Deputy Director of Intelligence and Foreign Affairs, gestured for them to sit. The room was packed. A high chrome table and white leather chairs filled the small meeting area. It was unexpected. The glass table had a tablet laid in front of each seat.

"Please come in and take a seat. Please."

"Nice to finally meet you, Ms. Oliver; please call me Ian." Jill gave Ian a half-smile and sat directly across from him and another man, much thinner than Ian, named Todd Bower. David sat beside her, and Ian began. "It's late... well, early, but we thought it best to move fast." The two men picked up their tablets and appeared to be logging in with a fingerprint sign-in. "Well, it looks like we found a mole," he said, glancing down at the screen. "Allan Mars. Age thirty-four. Research Assistant for the CIA. We're astonished by this, and frankly, we have a hard time imagining him as our mole. I've read the brief from Paul Grant that just came in. I've worked with Allan on different assignments. It's hard to believe," he said, shaking his head slowly. "We're working on investigating him further. We should know more about his motives by the end of the day."

Todd added, "The question is more for you, David," he said. "We'll need a full report in detail about what happened. Shame you killed him. It would have been better for our intel if he'd been alive. Whatever were you thinking? Why did you use excessive force?"

Jill looked over at David, watching his response. "I didn't mean to kill him. It's just that I had to gain control of the vehicle. We were going about fifty miles an hour."

"Why did you take control at that time? Why not wait until you stopped?"

David shifted slightly. "Is there a problem here?" Todd returned a poker-faced stare. David looked from one to the other. "Look, I gained control of the vehicle by pounding his face into the steering wheel. I got control but used too much force, I guess; it wasn't intentional."

This response bewildered Jill. Why did he lie to these two guys?

Todd gave him a sly I-don't-believe-you glance before Ian spoke. It appeared Ian was taking notes by tapping on the tablet screen. He said, "Just make sure it's all in the report. We've recovered him, and it states here"—Ian swiped the screen—"the probable cause of death was head trauma, but we won't know for at least a week. Things don't get done fast here, you know." They swiped their tablets in unison.

Ian nodded and said, "The Gladios..." Jill noticed Todd shift at the mention of the words. She knew body language, and Jill sensed something was off-kilter. Todd looked down, avoiding David's eyes. "It's more than the Gladios, we believe. They're known thugs for hire these days," Ian said as he swiped again. "We've been following the chatter on the Turkish National Intelligence Organization. There's talk about a large shipment of heroin arriving or that has already arrived, maybe through Agri, Van, or Hakkari. They're the least guarded routes. You know how chatter is; they purposely let us eavesdrop to keep us off a solid trail. It makes actual intel tracking virtually impossible." Ian looked up at Jill and crafted a sideways smile as he moved his eyes from hers and down her body. Jill gave him an are-you-serious look, pushing his eyes back to the brief.

"Sorry to interrupt, Ian," Todd said, "but I still want to hear why Brown here knew for a fact that Allan was our mole. It just doesn't compute. For one, he didn't have the clearance for some of these susceptible documents." Todd looked at David before looking back at Ian. "Nor was he in Afghanistan recently. And frankly, why do something stupid when we knew he was extracting you from the safe house because of HUMINT?"

Jill moved her attention from them to David. She was interested in his answer too. Her eyes willed David to say something to help her understand.

David didn't respond to him. He looked at them and said flatly, "It will all be in my report. Can we move on? The sun's already up."

The two men gave each other a nod and then looked back at David. Ian spoke next. "Our initial HUMINT is telling us that the shipment of heroin is being organized by a different group, not the Gladios. Well, they may have a hand in organizing. I don't think they care how they make their money. Nothing definite on who yet, but the intel is pointing to one of our shipping ports for distribution."

Jill piped in. "Where's the shipment going?" Jill could feel Todd studying her.

Ian continued the brief, looking annoyed at the interruption. "Turkey is a global shipping hub. It's been a vital port since the sixties. And because of the sheer volume of routes, we do not have the human resources to inspect them all. But with the size of this shipment, it could only be going through a select few: Mersin, Nemrut Bay, and Dardanelles Strait. Our team is investigating those locations now."

"With all due respect, gentlemen," Jill interrupted as her questions tumbled out. "What does this shipment have to do with me? Do you have intel on who was following me? Do you know why I'm even here—Moneyval? You said Allan was a mole. A mole for who? The Gladios?"

Ian looked at Todd and nodded. "That's our question too, Miss Oliver. If it is indeed the Gladios following you, we'd also like to know why." Todd looked straight at David as he finished his sentence.

Ian interjected. "But at this point, we do not have any more information. Originally, your assignment was to profile the Moneyval staff to determine if their reports were falsified or fabricated. Their findings will play a big role in what our governments—Turkey and the US—will do with this war on terror. We want to know how effectively the coup took out the president of Turkey. But your assignment was pulled after last night's events. I'm afraid we will not know if the audit of their findings at the emergency summit is legit. We have a NOC or two in there, but they're low-grade security cleared. Given your background and recent catapult in your career, you would have been perfect. We've heard good things about you." Ian continued, "But for now, you both must stay in our secure extension of the Embassy. Just until things are sorted."

"Until the autopsy report comes back," Todd blurted.

CHAPTER
TWENTY-NINE

Sunlight shone on one edge of the black leather couch, warming it. The smell of freshly brewed coffee lingered in the air. Jill sat, feeling perplexed. "This is ridiculous, David. I mean, something... something just isn't adding up." Questions spun around in Jill's head faster than a category-seven tornado. She got up and poured herself another cup of coffee. "What?" Jill said as she stopped and looked at David.

"What do you mean... what?"

"Why are you looking at me like that?"

"Like what?" A pause. "How am I looking at you?" David said with a slight sigh.

Jill looked around the room, scanning for any surveillance equipment. She spied none. "Didn't you think it was strange? I mean, in the meeting, they seemed disinterested. Like they had more information than what they were telling us." David looked at her intensely, and Jill went on. "Don't you think they were just placating us? For goddamn sakes, I've been almost kidnapped, and you've been shot at, and we've been chased around Istanbul. You apparently accidentally killed Allan because of a hunch. Why didn't you tell them the truth about how

Allan was killed? They will discover that smashing his face in didn't cause his death. What else is going on?"

Jill sat and waited for a response, but she couldn't help herself; she had to continue. "To me, they were more interested in Allan than in finding heroin. They seemed more interested in us. Like we committed a crime or something. Frankly, I don't even think the commander knows what the hell is going on."

"Trust me, Jill, he does."

"Are we prisoners here? It sure feels like we are under suspicion for something." David was about to interject, but Jill continued. "If Allan's giving HUMINT to the Gladios, my question is why. Why would they think you or me, for that matter, know something about a big shipment of drugs?" Jill watched David's eyes. "I mean, why would they think you know anything at all?" She waited for some sort of recognition, some kind of sign—David remained poker-faced. Silence filled the room in the pregnant pause before Jill picked up her bag. "We need to talk to someone about that girl. And then"—Jill turned back toward David—"I need to rest and get the hell away from you."

CHAPTER THIRTY

"Tt. Tt. Tt," Matthew McGregor stuttered as he rocked. The gray cement walls were chipped inside his cell, as if he had picked at pieces of bubbled paint for a long time. Matthew sat cross-legged on the floor in front of the cell bars that held him captive.

"Is this all he has been doing?" the doctor asked the corrections officer. The doctor returned the file to the guard, turned, and stood directly before Alfred Maxter. "It states that you are on the list for disclosure. I'm not sure why he'd want a journalist to know about his episodes or his diagnosis."

"With all due respect, doc, it's there in black and white. Why he wants the world to know about him to this depth? It's not for you to be concerned about," said Alfred.

The doctor studied him, then pushed past him and began to walk. "I'm busy right now, so if you must know more about his condition, you must walk with me." The doctor moved fast, and Alfred had trouble keeping up with him.

They waited for the guard to unlock the hallway door. Once they were on the other side of the door, the doctor continued moving forward. "Since yesterday, this is all that he does. He hasn't been eating. Hasn't been sleeping. To the best of my knowledge, he's just been rocking and stuttering, tt-tt-tt. Who the hell knows what that's all about? I've been told you were the last person to speak with him two days ago. What did you talk about? It could have been something that triggered his current state. He's got dissociative identity disorder. It's a severe form of dissociation. Probably from some trauma as a child."

"Well, Mr. McGregor did ask for me to get in touch with his half-sister. Her name is Jill Oliver. But... but I told him that she wouldn't speak with him. She's in Europe somewhere now. When I said this, he... well... he freaked out. They started talking in different voices. It was wild. I haven't been able to sleep much since." Alfred huffed, trying to keep up with the doctor's gait. "I guess it makes sense if he has that mental dis—"

The doctor stopped, and Alfred bumped into the back of him. "Dissociative identity disorder." The doctor looked like he wanted to stomp on Alfred as if he were a cockroach and said, "You do know the man's history, don't you? You're an author; have you not done any research? You know how he killed those people, how he killed his mother? Tell me you at least know that?" He continued walking.

Alfred nodded and followed. "I do. He killed his mother when he was twelve, then started a killing spree after he was released from custody."

"He murdered his mother with an ice pick to the face."

"Yes, I know that," Alfred said, a little out of breath. "But I don't understand why he needs to find Ms. Oliver so badly. He almost killed her too. You can understand why she doesn't want to be found by him."

The doctor abruptly stopped again. "Okay, I'm not one to push for the rehabilitation of a person who can't be cured. No medication can help him. But he can reduce his episodes if he is committed to his meds." The doctor hesitated. "So you're saying that when you mentioned his half-sister, this was when he reacted?" Alfred nodded hesitantly.

"Okay, let's go back and test this theory. I'm curious to note this in my findings, anyway. Let's see his reaction when I ask him." The doctor turned and returned to the locked hallway door leading to Matthew's prison cell.

The guard buzzed the door open, and they walked through. The doctor marched to Matthew's cell and stopped. Matthew rocked back and forth. Back and forth. Looking over to Alfred, the doctor said, "What was her name again? This sister?"

"Jill Oliver."

Instantly, Matthew stopped rocking; he did not move. He just stared at the ground. The doctor sighed, looked at his watch, then sighed again.

Matthew scrambled, pulling himself up onto his feet. The chains rattled hard against the bars as he let out a guttural scream. Sprays of spittle flew through the bars when Matthew squished his head in a here's-Johnny-Shining moment. "Find her," he growled. "Find her, or you are dead." And with one swift motion, Matthew punched his fist between the bars, startling the doctor. Alfred stumbled backward, almost tripping, and dropped his notebook.

"Get out of here," the doctor said. "I've had enough."

CHAPTER
THIRTY-ONE

Jill followed David. She hadn't wanted to see him this soon—hadn't wanted to speak to him. But David had gotten a meeting with one of the women who had been with the little girl, and for that, Jill was thankful. Why did she care so much about this girl? She hadn't answered that question, but she sure as hell would find out if the girl were okay. Perhaps she was projecting onto this girl, trying to evade thoughts of her childhood—a distraction, maybe. But Jill didn't want to think about that now. She had to find a deep emotional spot in her psyche that would give her the coping mechanism to deal with those memories, and she wasn't about to do that anytime soon. But she knew. She had learned from what happened to her in the months after her captivity with Matthew. She knew they would come barreling in. They always did. For now, there was this girl. Distraction was just what she needed right now.

The sound of boots echoed as Jill and David made their way to the meeting. David managed to find the intake deputy on shift last night. They stopped short of entering her office. The plaque on the side of the doorway read Yasmin Al Bout—Intake Deputy. "Why don't you do it now? I'm tired of hearing excuses," the woman barked into the black mobile phone in broken English. Her brown eyes narrowed as Jill and David entered the room.

The room was stark. There was no personality for Jill to profile. Two small photos of old villages hung behind the woman on the phone. They were slightly off-kilter on the dull yellow cement walls. The morning seeped between the white blinds, attempting to soften the room.

Jill watched as the woman's right brow furrowed, pulling the left one into a full-blown scowl. "Just get it done! This is your last warning, and if the car is not washed by the time my shift is over, I'll have your sorry ass on the next flight back to Ethiopia." The color of her face moved from flushed to a bright cherry red. She had mousy brown, bone-straight hair that tapped her shoulders. "And this time, I will ban your return to Turkey so you cannot put any other families here through such incompetence." She jabbed the phone screen with her index finger before throwing it onto the desk.

A waft of musk hit Jill's nose. The woman's face bubbled with moisture as she stood. "You must be David Brown?" she recovered coyly. "They said you needed to see me urgently."

David nodded and said, "Yes, this is Jill Oliver."

The woman gave Jill a blank stare and then looked back at David. "Please sit," she softly commanded, pulling on her short, tight black suit jacket before sitting back down.

David spoke first. "We're here to inquire about a girl."

"Oh?" Her left brow lifted.

"The one that was in the holding area earlier. Do you remember me?" Jill asked.

The woman looked at Jill and then back at David. "What girl?"

This action pissed Jill off, and she interrupted the woman. "There was a girl in the holding area. She was wrapped in a blue blanket. Where is she now?"

The woman shrugged, evading Jill's glare, and gave David a flirty smile. "It's complicated."

"Complicated? What do you mean it's complicated?" Jill said pointedly to the woman. Jill looked over at David. "Can't you call someone, David? Get them to tell her it's okay to share this information." Jill glared back in the woman's direction. She was annoyed now with this woman's demure and careless response. Jill's blood temperature rose, and before waiting for David's response, she told the woman, "Can you at least tell us where she is? Who is she? Her name?"

The woman looked over at David, whose back was turned to both of them. He spoke in a hushed tone when he turned and said, "Here," pushing his mobile into the woman's face.

Ms. Al Bout gingerly took the phone and listened. After several nods and a yes, she hurriedly handed the phone back to him. "Please wait," she softly spoke and stood.

A minute later, the woman returned to the room and placed a folder on her desk before sitting back down. She flipped the file open with the tip of her bright red, fake fingernail and looked up. "I'm curious. Why do you care about this girl? She's probably just a poor runaway."

Jill leaned forward. "Why do you say that? What makes you think she's a runaway?" It was at this point that Jill began to despise the woman. Her sheer disregard for a child was inexcusable. Overdone makeup. Too-tight clothes. As she walked, one shoe heel tapped out a much-needed Morse code for a cobbler on the concrete floor. Her rudeness to whoever was on the other end of the phone was telling. Some public servant, Jill thought. What a hobo bitch. "What did you say your name was again?" Jill looked at the gold plaque on her desk, which read Yasmin Al Bout—Intake Deputy.

The woman caught the slight and ignored the question. Instead, she began to recite what was in the file. "Gabriella Smith. Twelve-year-old girl. Said she was from Italy but is American. Her parents' names were Sophia and James Smith."

"Were? What happened to her parents?" Jill questioned.

"Said both her parents had died and that she was sent here from Italy by a cousin to go to boarding school." The woman hesitated, then continued. "The boarding school was not a boarding school. She said she was beaten and repeatedly raped." The woman stopped, looked up at them, and continued without emotion, "Here in Turkey, there are many runaways. Money is hard to find these days, and some people are destitute. There are plenty of brothels in Istanbul."

"With children who are twelve claiming to be American? Don't you find that odd?" Jill asked. The woman crossed her arms and was about to speak when Jill dismissed her idiotic opinions and raised her voice. "How was her English? How did she end up in Turkey if she lived in Italy? Did she say anything else?"

"She spoke excellent English."

"Didn't that seem strange to you? Did you call the police to shut down the brothel?"

"It is not our job to get involved in local governance. We are an American Embassy, not Turkish." She glowered.

David nudged Jill with his foot. "Can you tell us anything else about her?"

"She just seemed agitated... afraid. She kept reciting a number. Over and over." The woman looked back to the lone page in the file. "1376833626."

"A number, that's it, just a number? She didn't say anything else?" David queried.

Ms. Al Bout shook her head. "It's all in the file. You read it," she said, annoyance clear in her tone. She pushed the file in front of him. She gave Jill a blank stare and stood fast. David reacted by standing up. And as he did, it gave Jill the opportunity she was waiting for. Jill leaned in as David unintentionally distracted Ms. Al Bout and took a photo of the page.

"Look, I'm just the intake person here," said Ms. Al Bout. "We see many individuals coming to the Embassy claiming all sorts of sad stories. I lost my job. I can't afford to get back to the US. Blah, blah, blah." She crossed her arms; her head was slightly tilted. "My job is to record the intake details and delegate them to a caseworker." She grabbed the folder off the desk and moved towards the door.

"Look, Ms. Al Bout," David said gently but firmly. "Please sit down. We're sorry. Please. Please sit down."

She let out a huff but returned to her chair.

"Who is the girl's caseworker? How can we reach this person?" David asked.

The woman shrugged nonchalantly. "I don't know."

Jill glared. "What do you mean you don't know?"

She shrugged again. "A woman from CACU, Crimes Against Children Unit, showed up before I could call anyone. Given the girl's age, I figured the duty clerk must have called." Her lips wrinkled, and with a slight hesitation, she reached for the folder, opened it, and scrolled to the bottom of the page. "A woman named Rana Al Ahmed signed for her. See." She turned the file in their direction.

Jill and David looked down at the signature.

"Did she have an ID?" Jill pushed back, her voice slightly louder.

"Of course, she had ID. Everyone who comes into the Embassy has an ID. The duty clerk would have checked it. Recorded it."

"But you didn't see any ID?" Jill persisted.

The woman shook her head, closing the file.

Jill didn't know if her exasperation was about everything that had happened to her since she found out David was alive. She didn't know if it was jetlag or the fact that some sinister group called the Gladios was trying to capture her. She didn't have a goddamn clue why she said what she said next. All Jill knew was her anger was so strong it had exploded into rage. And then it happened. The ringing in her ears, attempting to overpower her voice, pushed Jill over the line. "You mean to tell me that you just let a twelve-year-old child leave with a stranger after the girl said she was captured, beaten, and raped in a boarding school nearby?" Jill's voice boomed as her fury elevated. "You're telling me... You're telling me that you didn't even check her goddamn ID?"

Everyone was standing now. Ms. Al Bout moved to the door. "Look, I don't like what you're insinuating. I did my job. This is all I know. If you want to learn more, check with the duty clerk." She slammed the heavy wooden door as she left the room.

David looked over at Jill, watching her try to wrestle her bag from the chair. She slung it over her shoulder. "What a bitch!"

David showed no emotion. He just stared at Jill. He lifted his hands, palms facing Jill, and in the calmest voice said, "Jill..."

But she interrupted. "For Christ's sake, David. Not you too." She marched past him and opened the door. Looking back at David, she said, "Where the hell is the duty clerk?"

She didn't wait for an answer as she stalked from the room, leaving David to trail after her.

CHAPTER
THIRTY-TWO

Jill continued down the hall. David caught up to her. "Jill, why are you so worried about this girl? It's all SOP, standard operating procedure. I'm sure proper protocol has been followed. The girl is probably sound asleep after a long bath in a children's shelter or safe home or something. Why do you care so much about her?" His voice trailed off as he kept her pace. "I mean, I can imagine what that girl has gone through. If it's true, and all."

Jill turned quickly and was about to say something she'd regret. Then, as if a light switch flicked on, she recanted her thought and moved her arm like a waiter escorting someone to a table. Jill knew that she'd need to be calmer if she wanted to get David's help right now. She needed to get the answers. The thought stung her, but he had the clearance. She had nothing. Not even her assignment with Europol anymore.

She turned and walked with David to the bulletproof glass speckled with air holes. Behind it sat a small man. David flashed his lanyard that announced his security clearance. The man pointed to a metal tray that slid out from the glass. David placed the lanyard in, and the tray snapped shut. The man studied the ID before sending it back through to David. In broken English, he said, "How can I assist you today, Mr. Brown?"

David leaned his head forward, getting closer to the holes. "A Rana Al Ahmed was here earlier. Did she leave her ID number or mobile number? She was from CACU—you know, the Crime Against Children Unit?"

The man looked down, skimming the log. His glasses pushed up and down his nose when he spoke. "No one has signed in under that name. No one from CACU has signed in at all."

Jill choked out a cough. But David spoke first. "Are you sure? There was a girl here last night."

"She was sitting over there," Jill interjected.

The man looked over in the direction of where Jill's finger pointed. "Oh, I see. You would not normally have to sign in to sit there, only if you go into the Embassy." He turned and pointed to a locked door leading to a security corridor where you'd stand. When one door opened, the other was locked. "Otherwise, it's more of a waiting room." The man chuckled softly. "I don't know how often I explain this to people," he murmured.

David gave Jill a puzzled look, and Jill could see that he understood her instinctive reaction. "So there is no way to find out who this Rana Al Ahmed is?"

He shrugged. "Why are you so concerned? Was there a crime committed?"

Jill pushed in front of David. "Look, Mr. eh... Mr.—" She searched for a nameplate or something. "A child has been taken from the US Embassy. An American citizen. You mean to tell me you can't help identify who took a twelve-year-old girl from here?"

The man frowned and then said, "We could pull the video feed, but you'd have to have special permission from the powers that be for something like that. I am not authorized to do that." He hesitated and appeared to be thinking of a solution. "You said, twelve-year-old girl? When was this?"

"About eight hours ago."

"Can I get your contact details? It will take some time to get this approved."

"Time?" Jill stammered. "How much time? How long will it take to find a child taken from US soil? For all we know, she was kidnapped!"

The man gave Jill an eye roll. David recited his email to the man and pulled Jill away by the elbow.

"Mr. Brown. Wait!" the duty clerk chirped and nodded, gesturing for David to come to the holed wall.

David turned, let go of Jill, and walked over. Jill watched as the men conversed, and then the clerk slipped a small brown envelope to David via the tray and gave Jill a nervous stare. David picked it up, looked at Jill, ripped the edge, and pulled out a note. He read it and pushed it back into the envelope.

Jill moved toward him. "What? What is it?"

"It's just a note from a colleague asking me to contact them."

"Them? Who's them? How did they know to find you here?"

"I guess they must have tried my number. Remember, my phone got stomped on at the safe house. Anyway, don't worry your pretty head about it, Jill. It's just a colleague."

CHAPTER
THIRTY-THREE

The embassy residence wasn't Shangri-La, but it did give the feeling of being in a hotel. There was a desk, a bed, and, more importantly, a minibar. David's room was across the hall. Jill was happy to have her space, especially considering what she had learned in the past twenty-four hours. Besides, she needed some time alone, away from David—she needed some time in the tunnels. Jill leaned over, opened the minibar, and took out a mini bottle of Glenfiddich scotch. She grabbed a glass, poured out the contents of the bottle, which was only a finger-sized measure, and held it up in the air. "Cheers, David!" she said and shot back the drink.

She reached into her bag, pulled out her laptop and leather pouch, and placed them on the table. She set a bottle of water and a fresh glass down beside them. After turning on the laptop, Jill poured the water and logged into her VPN. She pulled up her inbox.

Hello Jill,

I trust this email finds you safe and sound. I received your voicemail. Please call me on a secure line as I have some new developments to discuss with you.

Eric

"There are new developments, alright." She glanced at the clock. It would be 8:30 a.m. EST in Virginia. Eric should be up. She contemplated the call. What was she going to say to him? She was told not to mention to anyone that David was alive. Well, that's what David had told her. But it was Eric, after all. He was there for her during her stint at the FBI. He was her father figure since she didn't have one. He loved her that way, too, especially after Matthew McGregor. Jill knew he felt guilty about what happened to her. He was her direct boss who commissioned the Remote Viewing team to find the

Iceman.Jill sighed. She'd play it by ear, and since he asked her to call him on a secure line, no one would know what they talked about. Jill thought about it. A minute passed, and she tapped on the VPN Washington link with the mouse. A cogwheel turned as it attempted to add another layer of security before letting her know that she was logged in. She double-clicked the voice-over-IP dialer, and a phone pad filled the screen. She hit speed dial seven, Eric's mobile. Two rings, then, "Wallace." Hearing his voice made Jill smile. A little bubble of calmness surrounded her.

"Eric, it's Jill. The line's secure."

A quick pause from the network delay, then, "How's Turkey? How are you settling in? Is Europol as good as it's been bragged it would be?" His questions tumbled in.

"I'm not sure, Eric. I haven't seen anyone yet." Silence filled the connection. "Hey, do you have security clearance for what I'm doing in Turkey? I mean, do you know why I'm here?"

"No, I'm busy with the Remote View assignments. We're still training more analysts right now. Oh, and Mitch says hello. Is everything good?"

"Well... yeah, it's all good." She hesitated. A lump of guilt balled up inside. "Say hi back."

"Everything okay?"

Jill didn't answer for a moment. "Your email told me you had some new developments," she said too matter-of-factly. She'd have to be careful since Eric knew that was one of her coping skills. When Jill was under too much pressure, she'd become super professional. "Sorry, Eric, I'm just a bit tired. It's probably just the jet lag."

"Can you tell me where you're staying?"

Jill looked around the room. "Not much to say, some sort of residence. It's attached to the American Embassy. Everything's secret around here." That statement wasn't far from the truth. But it was Jill who was keeping the most secrets from a man she adored. She realized too late that Eric knew only high-risk cases would put people in an Embassy residence. To his credit, he didn't query the slip.

A pause hung before Eric said, "Have you heard about Stan Brown?"

"Huh? No, what?"

"I had drinks with someone in the know last night. I can't say who, but he had some intel from Guantanamo Bay. Are you sitting down?"

Jill wondered if Stan had finally cracked. Maybe it would be Stan Brown who exposed David's involvement in the now-thwarted plot. How ironic would that be?

Eric went on. "Turns out Stan Brown is dead." Jill sucked in a quick breath. "Killed himself with his pillowcase—hung himself from his bed rail."

"Eric, hang on." She walked over to the minibar and grabbed a mini wine bottle. She cracked it open, sat back down, and poured. "Are you sure? Was this verified? Was it really a suicide?" Jill knew Stan was a bastard, a coward, but she didn't think suicide would be part of his makeup, and she couldn't picture how he could even accomplish this with his size. "Do they have a body? Do they have proof?"

"I didn't ask that. Of course, they would have one; it would be obvious. Dead guys don't get up and walk away. That's a weird question."

Jill's thoughts trailed off, thinking of David. She thought hard about telling Eric that David was alive and in Turkey. The idea made the ball in her stomach start to blister. She sighed and took a drink of wine.

"I know you think he's responsible for David's death, Jill, but he's dead now. Story over. You can close the book and move forward." Jill didn't speak. "Jill, you okay?"

Guilt was now bubbling up her esophagus. "Yeah, I'm okay." Thoughts of the time Eric came to see her after Matthew McGregor and her childhood discovery were pushing in again.

Jill slayed her guilt with another gulp of wine. Besides, what would she say to him anyway? Hey, Eric, David's alive, and we are being hunted by some sort of Gladio operation that may be connected to a heroin shipment. Some thugs tried to take me twice in the past twenty-four hours. Even thinking of what she would say made Jill wonder about the circumstances she was currently in. David. Turkey. Stan's death. Were they connected?

She knew that if she told Eric any of it, he would worry about her. Besides, she didn't know exactly what was happening, but she was damn sure she was going to find out. She locked her thoughts away in one of her mind's compartments. She'd deal with those feelings later. "I'm good, Eric. Truly I am." More silence.

Eric breathed a little too forcefully. "I got your message, but there's one more thing first... have you talked to Kali lately?"

"Yeah, I talked to her yesterday. Why?"

"So she told you about McGregor wanting to get in touch with you."

A shudder rumbled through Jill. "Yeah," she whispered.

"Well, this author guy showed up at her office."

"What! She didn't tell me that."

"I guess he was a bit, you know, agitated. He seemed desperate to speak to you and, at the very least, give you a message." Silence hogged the line. "Kali called me. She didn't know if she should tell you about it. I told her I'd call you since I had to return your call anyway."

Jill wondered why Kali would feel this way. After all, even though Kali was her researcher, she was also a good friend. The only thing that would stop her from calling was that it must be awful news. "What was the message?"

"It was a weird message, Jill, and I had to repeat it back to her as it didn't make much sense. Gibberish, actually."

"What was it?"

"The author said that McGregor was demanding to speak with you—that he was becoming violent. Kali said this writer guy seemed afraid."

Jill pushed back. "Well, there is nothing to be scared of. He's locked up for life. Serves this author guy right. The guy's an idiot for getting involved with a serial killer. I have no sympathy, and I don't care right now."

Eric interrupted. "What he kept saying was odd, though. He kept saying t, t."

"T, t?" Jill simmered down and listened.

"Yeah. T, t, over and over, I guess," Eric confirmed.

"That is odd," Jill opened her notebook to the page she was working on, wrote it down, and circled it. "The guy's a crazy psychopath. Who cares?" But something about what she wrote gave Jill some pause.

She traced the two t's as Eric continued. "Anyway, I think you should get any information about him and this author guy. I've asked Kali not to hold back anything. It's part of your recovery to hear and talk about what happened. I just want what is best for you, Jill, and in my humble opinion, the only way is full disclosure. It's what Joan would have told you to do." Jill smiled sadly at the mention of Eric's late wife but didn't say anything.

"Anyway, you left a message, but there were no details," Eric said.

Jill finished her wine. "You remember David's colleague Leila. Leila Sorel?"

"Yes, I remember her. Well, we've never actually met."

Jill thought about that. She wondered if he had met her, would Leila have cast her spell on him? Leila often bragged she could cast spells.

"Why, Jill?"

"I'm not sure." Jill paused as her stomach began to clench. "Well … I've been thinking about some things. I mean, some things happened during the time she was helping me find David. Remember, during that period, I kept seeing the term 'family'—those dreams about my mother, my grandmother?"

"I remember you told me about those." Jill could picture his fatherly expression, which began to soften the grip on her gut. "I don't understand, Jill. What do those dreams have to do with Leila?"

For a moment, Jill felt silly. Was she really going to ask Eric? But it'd be him if she could ask anyone about her sometimes far-fetched theories. She had nothing to lose, really. She trusted Eric, and he knew her well. "Do you still have that contact in the CIA? You know—"

Eric interrupted, "Yes."

"Or maybe Johan could help…"

"What's this about, Jill?"

"I don't know how to explain it, Eric. I mean …"

"Have you been Remote Viewing again?"

"No, it's just... it's just something that keeps returning to me. It's just that... it's bugging me. Leila had met with Stan Brown before we met up in Hamburg. She had met him before she met up with me. Leila knew nothing of what I was doing or why I was in Hamburg. She met up with Stan in Brussels before I even got there. She said that Kali had told her I was in Hamburg, but the funny thing is, I hadn't called Kali until I landed."

"What is it you are saying?"

"It's just... I don't know." Holding the wine glass tighter than she should, her toe tapped against the leg of the desk. "It's just my—"

"Intuition," Eric finished.

"Yeah," Jill said quietly. "I guess it sounds... I don't know..." Jill huffed out her breath. "It didn't cross my mind until this trip to Turkey. You know... the tunnels." But Jill knew it wasn't just the tunnels; it was the presence of David that made Jill question things. Question everything about her husband. His job. His friends. His family. Everything. "Images just keep interrupting my thoughts, and I need to... I don't know. I know it doesn't make much sense. But there is something about Leila that won't give me peace." Jill paused, stopped her toe taps, and said, "Can you do some off-the-radar snooping? I mean... some simple inquiries about Leila, that's all. See if there are any red flags." Silence. "You think it's stupid." Jill lowered her head; her face was flushed.

"You know I would never think anything you do is stupid, Jill. I'm just wondering, what's this about? Stan?" Eric's voice lowered, and compassion flowed gently through his words. "Is this about David?"

She'd hoped the alcohol would have dulled the tinge of guilt that twisted tight again with the question. Nope, not today. Jill sucked at lying. She had a hard time even telling white lies. It's probably why she didn't have too many friends. Too many lies to keep up with. No one spoke for a few seconds; then Jill piped up in a cheery tone. "I'm okay, Eric, don't worry."

"I know you can't talk about your assignment. But I'm sure you'll have an interesting time when you get started."

Jill looked around the room and thought about Eric, about his strength. But even with that, he'd still worry about her. There wasn't much else for her to do but put on her best performance. "Things are quiet now, Eric; it's a bit boring at the moment." Taking a deep, silent breath before signing off, she said, "It's all good right now. It's all good."

CHAPTER
THIRTY-FOUR

Stan Brown is dead. Dead. Suicide. How convenient. But the burning question that ignited the fire attempting to boil Jill's blood was, if this happened several days ago, why hadn't David heard about it? Maybe he had, and it wasn't convenient for him to share this with her. Convenient. Jill pushed the empty glass away with too much force and almost knocked it over. She rubbed her finger over the mouse several times, opened Google, and searched "Stan Brown" using quotes for more condensed results.

The search pulled up several articles and even a link to his LinkedIn page that showed a professional picture of him with a serious look on his fat face. No mention of his death. She didn't dare click on the "read more" link. He was dead, and it was probably the last thing anyone would think about removing. Besides, Jill knew all social media activity was logged. She knew about packets and the storage of these packets for five years. She'd seen countless reports of who was using what keywords. The whole WikiLeaks publishing didn't change much.

What struck her as odd, though, was that there was no information about Stan's arrest last month in Abu Dhabi or even his transfer to the Bay. She supposed there might have been some media blackout;

there often was. But surely the alternative media folks would have been all over it. Come to think of it, Leila was the only person who had told her that Stan was sent to the Bay. "Shit," she said aloud. Her head was foggy, and so was her vision. She leaned back, closed her eyes, and wondered if she should have had that last glass of wine. Her tongue felt thick as she tried to run it over her new teeth. She hadn't done it in a very long time since she had them replaced after a brutal serial killer decided to smash her head into a cement floor. Matthew. Not Matthew again. Running her tongue over her teeth was a habit she had after she had gotten new ones. A sort of reminder of her real strength when she knew an attack was trying to creep in. She hadn't needed her security blanket rituals since David came into her life, anyway. She took several slow, deep breaths and tried to relax. She wanted to get into her intuitive

tunnels. Her deep, yoga-like breathing began to slow her mind. Slow enough to jump on that bobsled that would race her through her thoughts—through the recent events, looking for anything that was off. But it was different this time, maybe the booze. Damn. She kicked herself. She needed to zone out. Needed to hop on for the ride. But she couldn't. She thought about Gabriella. She thought of the meeting with the two deputy do-littles. She thought... she thought. She thought. Zen.

She was racing now, but usually, she'd only see one or two images for her to focus on. This time, there were too many pictures. Like kernels of corn popping into her mind. Leila. Leila in Hamburg. Leila in Dubai. Leila after they left Abu Dhabi. Leila.

"Bang!" Jill jolted upright and almost fell off the chair. Everything was black. Usually, her instinct would be to get in her ready stance. But she didn't have her bearings yet. She waited, her heart still pounding from the surprise sound. She didn't move; only her eyes scanned the room. There was nothing to see. She turned to her sleeping computer, reached over, found the mouse, and shook it. She half-expected someone to jump from the shadows just to finish her fine day. But when the screen blinked on, lighting up the room, it was empty. Jill stood and noticed shards of tiny glass fragments below the now burnt-out light. "Damn." She turned and walked to the door, flicked on the bathroom light that could illuminate a small village.

Jill sat down, tapped the glass off her notebook, and looked at the two t's circled. Next to it, Jill wrote the word "Leila," circled it, and began scribbling underneath.

Being in the tunnels was not at all like a Remote View, but she instinctively began to write in chronological order.

Leila met with Stan Brown in Brussels.

Leila had met Jill in Hamburg just hours after Jill had landed.

Jill tapped her pen and thought about these words. Leila was the only person who knew they were going to meet with Nasser, the intelligence broker, in Dubai before he was mysteriously killed. And it was Leila who went with Jill to see Zayed and knew what hospital he was in. He was now dead. What did it all mean, and why did it matter now?

Jill looked down at her notes. She hadn't heard from Leila in weeks. Now Stan was dead. Jill's shoulder twitched—or was it a niggle? It was something. "Keep going," she whispered.

It was Leila and only Leila who spoke about Stan's capture to Jill. She was the one who said he was extradited from Abu Dhabi to the Bay. It was Leila who had kept her abreast of any goings-on with Stan at the Bay. Did he actually go? Jill ruminated. But what about Eric's call just now? He said he spoke to a friend in the know. He didn't say who. She thought about her conversation with him. She supposed it would have been easy enough for someone to name-drop the news about Stan Brown, knowing that Eric was Jill's confidant. But why go to so much trouble if it was a coup? "Stan is dead," she repeated, this time out loud. Jill wrote the word "Stan" next to it, "dead," and began to deduce... and if Stan was never at the Bay, why tell Eric he was, and why say to him that he's now dead?

And then there was David. Jill found it ironic, considering that David was a journalist for one of the most prestigious magazines in the world. Surely he would have been told about his father's death. Surely. Jill leaned back in her chair again.

The meeting today was even more perplexing. It was as if they suspected David was lying about how Allan died—why David used excessive force. They both were told not to leave the Embassy residence. Was she a suspect? It wasn't the first time she considered this thought. Did they suspect that Jill and David both killed Allan? Why would they even believe that? She thought about what had happened in the truck and ran through scenarios. If they thought Jill helped kill Allan, how would that play out? One thing was for sure, David lied about how Allan died. The autopsy would show blunt-force trauma to the back of the skull. As David's report showed, it would also prove that Allan's head was not bashed into the steering wheel. David was no dummy. He knew this truth would come out in about a week. Jill tried to move her thoughts along but was stuck on that last one. She sat up and wrote on the page: "One week."

And then there was Gabriella Smith. Jill shrank, thinking about what this little girl must have gone through. How in the hell does an American girl end up in a brothel in Turkey and then—poof—just disappear? And with suspicion looming over them from the CIA, would David even get any intel or clearance to view the CCTV camera recordings? Jill picked up her mobile phone, swiped it on, and selected contacts. Even she didn't have David's number here in Turkey. Colleague? Who the hell was trying to reach him? And why hadn't Jill thought to get David's number from him? Thinking about it now, he never asked for Jill's mobile number either. Jill pulled out her personal phone and examined the cracked screen. Even if she charged it, she couldn't swipe on the screen to view anything.

Jill walked to the door and peered out the spy hole, looking directly across the hall at David's door. No light protruded from beneath the door's crack. She unlocked her security lock and was about to open her door, then stopped, turned, and looked at the clock: 23:07. Who was she kidding? No response from David meant that he didn't have any news about Gabriella, and he sure as hell wouldn't hear anything at this time of night. Jill surrendered to this thought and wondered if she should discuss not being able to leave the Embassy with him when she saw him. She thought about asking if he had heard any news about his father. She looked over at the bed; it was calling her. Nothing was urgent about giving David that news; no one seemed to care about a missing child. Jill surrendered to her exhaustion. She flicked off the light, stripped off her clothes, walked over to the bed, and slid under the crisp sheets.

She had to turn off her brain. She needed her space; she needed time to figure out what the hell was going on. But that would have to wait. Turn off, Stan. Turn off, Leila. Turn off, David. She closed her eyes and began to drift.

Her face stung. She cupped her raw cheeks with her hands. Large hands were shaking her—shaking the girl. "You will pay," he said in broken English, smacking her hard in the face again. She could taste the copper from her split lip.

"I'm sorry," she whimpered. She was only twelve, but even she knew if she showed fear and remorse, he'd go easy on her. Well, that's what the others had said. She wasn't acting or even calculating; she was afraid. The punch to her stomach knocked her backward, and she tumbled off her feet. He didn't have to put much force into his blows, as the girl weighed less than one hundred pounds. She lay whimpering on the cold cement floor, hoping he'd go away. He stepped toward her and was getting ready to kick her. Kick her hard. Suddenly, he started mumbling in slow motion. Mumbling. Mumbling. Mumbling.

Jill's eyes shot open. Blackness surrounded her—surrounded her dark thoughts. She heard it. Mumbling. Jill held her breath and listened. Was she awake? Was she dreaming? More murmurs. Talking. It was the sound of people talking. Men. It sounded like two of them. Maybe David? Jill flipped off her covers and tiptoed to the door, put her ear to it, and listened. Nothing. She stuck her right eye to the peephole, held her breath, and looked out. The voices had stopped. She couldn't see anything. No one was there—at least not through this fish-tank bubble lens.

A cough echoed throughout the hall unexpectedly. Instinct made her move fast. She sidestepped away from the door and ducked into the bathroom. She stood there naked and waited, wishing she had grabbed her clothes off the floor on her way to the door. She waited for the next sound. She waited. There were no more sounds, no more talking.

She contemplated what to do next. Who would be out there at this time of night, and why? Her first thought was the Gladios. But this was a well-guarded building. No one would get in. But then again, Gabriella had disappeared right under security's noses. Shit. She had to step cautiously, even if her paranoia was playing tricks again. Should she go for the clothes or use the element of surprise and scare the crap out of whoever was behind the door? But she had no weapons.

Scare them how? Jill looked down at her taut breasts; her hard nipples pointed slightly upward. She answered her question. Jill hastened into the dark room, found her pile of clothes, grabbed her shirt, and tugged on her pants. She was barefoot but didn't care; she didn't have time for that. Back at the door, Jill went to turn the lock. It wasn't locked. She grabbed the lever hard and twisted it. Jill took a silent breath, then sucked one back in and quickly pulled the door open. She held a fighting stance with her back to the door jamb. Her heart raced as she waited for whoever was in the hallway to make their move. Her arms were bent at ninety degrees, and she held her fists before her face to deflect any blow. Jill knew her best bet; the first offensive move would be to go for the groin or the knees. But no one came at her. No one was there.

Jill leaned forward and peered up and down the hall. Empty. She looked at David's door, stepped closer, bent over, and listened. There were no sounds. She considered knocking. She scanned the hallway again and down to her bare feet and wondered what time it was. Hell, she didn't even know if she had heard what she thought she had. Jill breathed a quiet sigh, turned, returned to her room, and locked the door behind her.

Jill sat back on the bed and took a deep breath, trying to ease her adrenal glands from squeezing more Red Bull-type juice. What was going on? She thought of the mumbling, the two men talking. She thought of her dream.

She walked over, grabbed the notebook, and wrote down the time on the same page she had begun earlier. She added to the page, "Gabriella Smith." As her pen crossed the "t" in "Smith," a thought kicked Jill in the butt.

CHAPTER
THIRTY-FIVE

Sunlight reflected off Jill's computer as dawn crawled through the window. Jill was busy tapping on the keyboard. She had yet to hear from David about accessing the video feed or a pending visit to CACU that they had discussed before parting ways last night. Jill wasn't waiting. Not after the horrific dream she had about Gabriella. Besides, Jill wondered where David even was after hearing voices in the hallway. Maybe it was David talking to his "colleague." She hoped she had heard them and hadn't imagined it. Jill considered this as she sipped the instant coffee she had just stirred. She searched CACU Crimes Against Children Unit, and as the cogwheel churned, she knew all she had to do was knock on David's door and get him to find her the number. Certainly, he could get the contact details of the person they needed to speak to. But Jill was miffed, her nose out of joint. Even though she needed time alone, why hadn't David at least tried to see her? Maybe he thought she needed time alone too, or maybe he just didn't care.

Jill looked down at the screen. Her IP must have told Google she was in Istanbul because when she clicked on the first link, she saw a royal-blue logo and text in Turkish: Mägo. After clicking "translate this page," Jill determined that the first in the search was a hotline for exploited children affiliated with CACU. Leaning back, she contemplated calling the 600 toll-free number. But what would Jill say? She didn't know anything about Gabriella except her name, Gabriella Smith. She could Google her, but she was too young for Facebook, and Jill doubted she'd find too much about a lost American girl in Turkey. But then again, with a few more taps, she Googled "Gabriella Smith" in quotes. She knew it was a long shot and was right—"No results found," blinked the screen. She tried again, adding "Itay" and "American girl lost." Several stories came back from the search. None of them were about Gabriella Smith.

Smith. A very common name for someone with the first name Gabriella. Somehow, they didn't seem to go together. She decided to give Facebook a shot. Nothing. Too bad about Facebook, she thought, and took another sip. It was the easiest way to find intel on most people these days. Jill recalled a case she was profiling at the US Marshals Service. When Jill failed to find information on someone she was profiling, she'd search Facebook. Most of the time, criminals wouldn't be listed. But every once in a while, she'd find someone dumb. Stupid, she thought to herself.

David was her only option to contact someone who might know where Gabriella was in CACU or where she was placed. Jill grabbed her makeup bag and carried it into the bathroom. As she glided on her mascara, she thought of Stan Brown again. David must know he's dead. Why he wouldn't mention this to her was perplexing. But everything was befuddled right now. She had to push him—profile David. It was evident to Jill now; something was amiss with him. She needed to study him better and see what he did next. It was clear that she could not trust him. "What's your endgame, David?" Jill said as she took one last look in the mirror and smacked her maroon-colored lips together.

There was still no sign of light around David's door, and a single cue card read "Do not disturb" in English and Turkish: Mägo. The card was not there before, Jill recalled. She hesitated before gently knocking. Seconds passed, and when she heard no movement, she knocked again. Nothing. She looked up and down the hall. Where was everyone? Something was wrong. Jill turned, hurried back into her room, grabbed her phone and bag, and left.

CHAPTER THIRTY-SIX

"Did you get it?" David queried Yildiz Aslan as they walked towards the lone table in a dark corner of the residence lobby. The green splattered paint on the brown walls masked the room's age. A small candle on the table gave just enough light in the shaded area.

Yildiz looked frail, but she didn't feel very frail. Her tall ballerina-type frame willowed as she walked with him. She wore a black pantsuit with a turtleneck tunic zipped up just below her chin. They sat down on opposite sides of the small wooden table. Dark strands of hair pinched out from Yildiz's loose black hijab that was elegantly tied around her head. Yildiz was beautiful and wore just enough makeup to show her feminine side. You couldn't tell she was lethal, even with her long eyelashes and subtle red lips. She knew how to kill. She'd done it before. But David Brown didn't know this, she thought. No one knew—well, no one knew until it was too late.

She studied David as she sipped her hot tea. He was a handsome blond man whose face held a little too much sun. Perhaps of Scandinavian descent, she thought as she considered him. She looked at his throat and calculated the strike distance. She evaluated more pressure points: his eyes, the base of his nose, the distance from her knee to his groin.

"Yes." She nodded and pushed the small envelope across the table to him.

David picked up the envelope, slipped out the photo, nodded, and then slipped it back inside. "I'm curious," Yildiz's tongue curled. "Why did you need a picture of this building?" Yildiz Aslan was a Turk and the daughter of one of the highest-ranked combat battalion's brigadier generals. Abdullah Ahmed was a proud Turk of Ottoman descent. He was tortured and killed for speaking against Erdogan, Turkey's current dictator. A Turkish government informant had betrayed him. He died for his belief in a sovereign Turkey. Yildiz was her father's daughter in every sense of the word. She followed him when he worked his real job for President Fahri, who presided over the Turkish Invasion of Cyprus. He'd taken her to his training sessions. It was there she learned the craft of Krav Maga, a brutal and efficient tactical combative self-defense system developed by the Israeli Defense Forces. She learned it well. She held an expert-level three, similar to a black belt in martial arts training. But this was only a tiny detail about Yildiz Aslan. More importantly for Yildiz was her home. She was proud of her country, Turkey. Yildiz was an independent Turkish intelligence broker—she was one of the best in her field.

Her job was simple, or so you would think: receive the assignment, find the intel, deliver the intel, and get paid.

"I think I know what you are looking for," she purred as one of her eyebrows lifted. "But I don't believe that you will find it there."

David slipped the picture out, flipped it over, and studied the address: 727 Ocshitler SK. Then he slowly pushed it back inside. He looked back at Yildiz as she continued. "I know they told you I am worth what they pay me." She took another sip. "Well, I am. Your boss pays me well. They don't pay me to ask questions, just to complete the task assigned. But again..." She lifted another eyebrow, slowly licked her lips, then blew on the hot tea. "To take a picture of buildings..." She hesitated and took another sip of the drink. "I am very expensive for such a task."

"What do you think I am looking for?" His poker face held her gaze.

Yildiz tilted her head. "The Gladios are very powerful here," she whispered. "If they find out that you are looking for them"—a beat—"it will not be good for you."

David crinkled the right side of his mouth and slightly tilted his head. "Well, then"—a mocking smile—"you'd best not let them know."

CHAPTER THIRTY-SEVEN

Jill thumbed the handle of the door that led to the makeshift lobby. A small desk was stuffed into the corner. A man sat tapping his mobile phone. "Excuse me." The man looked up; his eyes drooped with annoyance. "Sorry to interrupt, but have you seen anyone this morning? A tall guy, blond hair?"

He nodded in a direction. "Over there, behind that big pillar." Then he resumed his finger tapping.

Jill moved in the direction indicated. As she rounded the large stone pillar, she stopped at what she saw. David sat in conversation with a woman. A Muslim woman, that was clear based on how she was dressed. David saw Jill and said something to the woman as he began to stand. The woman nodded in Jill's direction, then turned in the opposite direction, over to the security booth, and signed herself out.

David watched Jill as she strode over to the table. "Mornin'," he said.

Jill pointed towards security. "Who was that?"

He looked in that direction. "Her name is Yildiz Aslan. She works for the agency. Come sit down." He gestured as he sat. Jill followed. "I asked her to check on a theory I have about something. She's independent. Local intelligence, sort of like a runner."

"Theory? What theory? About the people who are chasing us?" she said hotly.

"I... er," David looked at her inquisitively. "Wait. Are you jealous?"

The words bit into her like a fighting cat. It wasn't the fact that he was meeting with a woman that scratched at her heart. At least, she didn't think so. Why was she acting like a jealous female? Scorned maybe, but jealous... Jill breathed deeply, attempting to compose her feelings.

David's smile widened. "I've gotten the go-ahead for the tapes. They'll be ready for viewing in about an hour. We've also been cleared to go to CACU. We can go there first, then come back here to watch the tapes."

"What about the men following us? Is it safe for us to leave the building? They're letting us go?"

"We're going in stealth mode. Out the back, a car and driver are waiting. It's about twenty minutes from here. Are you hungry? We have some time to

kill."Jill sat at the table and waited for David, who was pouring coffee from the self-serve food bar. She watched him and wondered if he knew about Stan Brown. She thought about his theory, Yildiz, what he was working on, and if it had something to do with Stan.

David sat and pushed a cup across the table to her. "Careful, it's boiling." She looked at the steaming cup and noticed he had added cream—just enough, the way she liked it. "I was going to come up to your room and get you. What brought you down so early?" he asked.

Jill eyed the clock on the wall: 7:52. "Early? Was that you outside my room talking to someone? I heard people talking."

David's head tilted. "People talking? What did you hear?"

Jill shrugged. "By the time I opened the door, no one was there." She studied David's poker face and thought she saw a hint of relief. She took a sip of coffee and waited.

"You want something to eat? It's looking pretty dodgy. Tarts and stuff." She knew he was attempting to change the subject, so Jill thought it was the right time to ask.

"What are you working on? What's the relevance of this theory you have? It must be important to get another person to help you. And what kind of name is Yildiz, anyway?"

David leaned back, eyed Jill, and said, "It's just a hunch I have."

"About what?" Jill sipped. "About... the Gladios? About the mafia? About Allan and who he was working for?"

David watched Jill intently. "Well, yes and no."

Jill rolled her eyes. "So you're not going to tell me? Don't you think that I have the right to know since I'm involved?" Her voice rose.

David's brow furrowed slightly. "Please, Jill, keep your voice down." He looked around the room.

At that very moment, Jill wanted to tell David that Stan was dead, shoving it in his face. But for once, she thought better of it, and the pain of biting her tongue made her wince.

"You know, Jill, you will have to start trusting me again. I just can't tell you some things. Not yet, anyway." He looked directly into Jill's eyes. His eyes were melancholy. Jill's heart pinched. Shit. "Why don't we just focus on the girl today? Like... like, remember when we had that fight in Tucson and weren't talking to each other?" He smiled softly. "And that little boy came up to us at the café, and he lost his dog. What was the dog's name again?"

"Buddy."

"Yeah, Buddy. That was it. We spent the whole day looking for that damn dog."

Jill listened, remembering that their entire focus was on that lost puppy—they laughed later, not remembering what they had even spat about. She smiled and nodded.

"I know it's not the same, Jill. I know." His blue eyes aimed to pierce the armor that now surrounded her heart. "But what do you say? I know this girl is important to you—finding her, I mean."

What really could she say to that? She was no longer on assignment. She had nothing to solve except her marriage, her life, and whatever the hell was going on. But David was right. Focus on finding Gabriella. The other stuff, well, that was the game called life, wasn't it?

David shrugged. "So, tell me again why you are so interested in this girl, Jill."

"As I've told you, I am a bit hypersensitive to some things. I guess it's because of what happened with Matthew McGregor, or so I've been told, anyway."

David looked at Jill. "Matthew McGregor. I haven't heard his name coming from your mouth... well, pretty much never; once, you made me swear not to mention his name again when I first asked. I read some media stories when I met you, but it didn't seem necessary. Well, to me, anyway. You seemed fine. Normal. And I suppose I figured I'd wait for you to talk about it—talk about him—but you never did."

Jill took a sip of coffee and stared past David. "Well, it's not about him," she whispered, not looking up at David. David took a sip and waited. "It's called hypersensitive intuition."

"You mean your psychic magic or whatever you call it. Remote viewing, right?" By the look on his face, David knew as soon as he said it he shouldn't have.

"It's not magic, David, and no, I'm not talking about that either. The doctors told me after McGregor that the trauma of my experience brought... Well, it has enhanced this in me. But it wasn't McGregor, really. It was always there."

David looked perplexed. Jill paused and thought intensely about what she was about to disclose, then continued. "Her name was Angela. We were only fifteen. She was pretty much my best friend. Well, she and Willie. Anyway, one night, we snuck out and met at the playground. It's what the cool kids did. We'd climb out of the bedroom windows and wait in the park until our parents fell asleep, and then we'd go back home in the middle of the night. We weren't the coolest kids. We didn't go drink beer or get high or anything like that. We didn't do that. We did it more for just the rebel vibe. You know, kid stuff. No one knew. I lived with my grandparents." Jill sighed, looking down at her cup. "Well, no one knew until that night."

Jill looked up at David, who was intently listening, and she continued. "It was a Saturday night, and May is a hot month in Arizona. Anyway, we had planned for the three of us to meet in the usual playground spot. Willie was there when I arrived, but Angela hadn't shown up. We didn't have to text back then, so we just thought her parents caught her, or she changed her mind, or something like that. We hung out until around two a.m. and then went home." Jill tilted her head and looked at David. "We never saw her again."

"Why? What happened?"

"Nobody knew. She just never showed up. It was a big deal in our small town. They thought someone had taken her. We heard nothing, but a search party with dogs was around the lake. It's very touristy in Page with Lake Powell so close. Great fishing. I used to go bass fishing all the time with my grandparents. We'd make a day of it. Some we even had cooked up on my grandpapa's boat-rigged barbecue. Anyway, years passed, and I eventually moved away. I was working with the FBI when I came across her name. Angela Barren. It turned out that she had been held at the local motel that night until a man came and picked her up and took her to Las Vegas. She was held there until she was sold."

"Sold?"

"Sold! Like at a cattle auction. Sold to the highest bidder," Jill mocked.

"I'm sorry, Jill." David reached across and put his hand on Jill's.

"I guess at some point, she befriended an undercover officer in Vegas. She told him her story."

"So he rescued her?"

Jill shook her head. "He was too late. Before they could sting the operation, the brothel had moved. They found her dead. Beaten with a hot branding iron before they bashed her head in with it. I couldn't look at those pictures.

"But after Angela's disappearance, I never got over... how, after the morning she disappeared, I slept in as if nothing had happened. But I knew something was very wrong the moment she didn't show up. Why didn't I act upon this intuition? If Willie and I had gone to her house when she didn't show up..." Jill pulled her hand from David's. "If only we had spoken up that night, or even the next day, for that matter, they could have found her—could have saved her." The tragedy began to bloom over Jill's face.

"I've not heard this story before, Jill," David said, shifting. He paused. "So this is why this girl means so much to you?"

"It's the same feeling," Jill's voice rose slightly. "It's the same feeling I had the night Angela disappeared. My intuition told me that something was just not quite right that night." Jill leaned back and let out another sigh. She looked at David and thought about telling him about her dream, about the girl in it. She considered sharing details about her childhood before her grandparents adopted her, but she knew she didn't trust him, and Dr. Erin was the only person who knew about what happened in her youth. She wanted to keep it that way. Besides, she didn't know if her dreams had anything to do with Gabriella. Well, she hoped they didn't. "That's why I need to find out about her—to know she is safe. That's all."

David leaned back. "Well, this may be your lucky day. Come on." He grabbed her hand.

Seventeen minutes later, they stood before what looked like a church. It seemed out of place in this Muslim country.

"What's this place? It doesn't look like a government building," Jill said, doing her scans.

"My, my, Jill," he said in a sing-song voice, "I think there is much more than just your Remote Viewing skills you haven't told me about. I mean, when did you take surveillance training?"

Finishing her scan, she thought there was a lot about her that David didn't know. She looked at him and wondered again if he knew the news about Stan Brown. She looked up at the sign on the side of the building that read "Children's Aid Society CACU." She didn't answer his question. They opened the heavy wooden door and stepped inside. The receptionist sat behind a tall wooden desk. A lone security guard sat in a small cubbyhole behind her. She said something in Turkish and, with no response from them, switched to English. "Can I help you?" David took out his ID and asked to see the duty manager.

Minutes later, they sat before a middle-aged woman dressed in a neat brown suit. Her long, dark hair was styled into a nice tight bun. "Rana, you say? Her name was Rana?"

Jill nodded and turned her phone so the woman could see her snapshot. The woman studied the phone. "May I?" she said as she swiped the image, enlarging it. "Rana Al Ahmed," she said as she grabbed the desk phone from its cradle and dialed. Speaking in a language they couldn't understand, the woman studied them as she repeated the name into the phone. Nodding as she hung up the phone, she said, "We have no one by that name working for us."

Chapter
Thirty-Eight

The lounge looked brighter than when they first arrived the night before. A television on a cart had been wheeled in and braked directly in front of the sofa. Three VHS-style video tapes were stacked on top of the VCR.

"What do you mean she didn't come into work today?" Jill spat out the question, and David shrugged. "That's a bit fishy, don't you think? We question her, and she disappears and doesn't come in." Jill was remote-control challenged, and after fiddling with it for a few minutes, she tossed it to David. "Clearly, something is very wrong, David. Can't they contact her at home? It's a missing child, for God's sake. And why would she show us that document if it was fake? Does she think we're dumb?"

"That is perplexing, and I'm afraid only she can answer that. They're trying to find her now. Maybe she thought no one would care." David sounded appeasing as he plugged in the power to the VCR.

"Are you sure everything is on these tapes?"

"He said it was. But I don't know what we will get out of watching it. Perhaps we'll see that woman, Rana, to get some sort of identification. Hopefully, we'll discover something that will help you. Jill?" David looked at Jill. "Jill?" His voice lowered. "Jill?" David sat down next to her. "What's wrong?"

Jill stared blankly into her cup and thought of Gabriella. And she thought about what she had told David about Angela. Her childhood thoughts were pushing in. She had to stop them from bursting her brain—bursting her heart. She began to lift her cup, but the slight tremble in her hand warned her not to. "It's... it's just that this whole thing about the girl is not making sense. I see this child. Minutes later, she is gone. Two women were there and then gone too. We meet with that cow, Yasmin, and she shows us a forged document from some Rana chick that doesn't even work for CACU. It's disturbing, David. Doesn't it bother you?" Jill reached for her coffee but instead put both hands under the table.

He leaned back, studying her before he spoke. "Okay, there was a girl, right?" he said rhetorically. "You're sure you saw a girl, right, not like, say... an adult that looked younger?"

The question interrupted Jill's pending downward spiral. She snatched up the coffee cup and took a gulp. "Of course, there was a girl. You saw the paperwork." Jill muttered something inaudible as she put the cup down harder than necessary. "Yes,"—pushing her chin in David's direction—"I saw a girl; she was sobbing. She was afraid."

"What did she look like?"

"I didn't get a good look at her... she had dark brown hair, but I'm a hundred percent sure she was not an adult. She was a child, David." Jill's eyes began to narrow. "A twelve-year-old is still a child. Her birthday was on the sheet, remember."

David went silent and pressed the play button on the remote. The screen lit up with a replication of the waiting area in the Embassy. They sat in silence, watching the silent room on the screen.

They hadn't watched much of it when a tall man, whom Jill did not recognize, entered the room. Jill watched the video intently but turned as the man tapped David on the shoulder, leaned over, and whispered in his ear. David slightly stiffened, glancing in Jill's direction. The man turned and walked briskly out of the room. Jill clicked pause on the remote.

"What?" Jill snapped.

David looked at the TV screen, contemplating. "Eh, eh... It's... well, as I mentioned, I've been working on a theory, and I've just been told that one of my communication markers has just been pinged."

"Pinged? What does that mean?"

"It means something in my theory may be happening. You know, put into action. That sort of thing."

"Does it have to do with the Gladios?" Her face turned from annoyance to interest. She wondered if this news had something to do with Stan Brown's death. Maybe this was a good time to ask him how much he knew about it. But first, she needed more information. "When will you tell me about this theory of yours, David?"

"I don't know," he said. "I need to be sure first."

It was that answer that made Jill decide that disclosing Stan's death to David now was not the right time. Besides, maybe he knew already. Who cared anyway if he was dead? This cat-and-mouse bullshit was pissing her off. Jill raised the remote and pointed it at the TV. David didn't say anything. He just nodded, urging Jill to press play.

The screen jumped and continued.

"Can you fast forward?" he said impatiently. Jill huffed and pressed the fast-forward button. Images blurred quickly across the screen, showing a relatively slow day and night at the Embassy.

"There," Jill said excitedly as she clicked the play button, slowing down the scenes. There was no sound, but it was clear. On the screen, two women stood in the corner talking to one another. One of the women was Yasmin, who they had met with yesterday—the one who was currently AWOL. The other woman's back was to the camera. They watched as the women appeared to be in a discussion. There was no sign of anyone else. Exasperated, Jill stood and walked to the television and crouched down. Pausing the video, she leaned forward and touched the bottom left of the screen. "See that?"

David stood and leaned towards the screen. "It looks like two bare feet popping out of a blue blanket."

Jill pressed play. There was barely any movement. Just ten little toes on dirty, sore red feet. Movement from the left of the screen captured their attention. "See, that's me." The display caught a fatigued Jill as she walked past the girl. "There must be more footage of the girl."

"Keep it playing."

They watched Jill cross the room and leave the area. A minute later, both women moved toward the child's feet, and one of them stopped. The camera was mounted above the child's head, and with its angle, it only captured the top of the woman's head. Then there it was. It was just a flicker. Jill reacted fast, pressing pause. On the screen was a vague outline, a glimpse of a person. A girl. Her small, sad face looked directly into the camera.

"There. See. That's her. That's the girl." Relief began to envelop Jill. The confirmation was settling her unrest that she indeed saw this girl. It was the girl, alright, and the same face that was in Jill's dreams.

"Hmmm, it's unclear, but it's definitely a younger female."

"I told you she was there."

David glanced at his mobile, checked the time, and said, "Let's continue watching." But the girl was gone from the scene now. They waited for a few more minutes before turning the video off.

"What do we do now, David? She was there; you saw her. If they think she went to CACU, they're mistaken; you know that."

David nodded and looked at his phone again.

"What, you have somewhere to go? Something more important than a missing child? Your theory again?" Jill stood, jabbing her hands on her hips.

David sighed as he stood directly in front of her. "Yes, she was here, Jill; the question remains, though. Why would anyone, especially someone without authority, take a child from the American Embassy in Turkey? It has to be legit, Jill. I know there is human trafficking everywhere, but this is the American Embassy. You'd need a big pair of balls to plan and execute something like that." He held Jill's eyes steadily. "Here's what we'll do. I'll call the Commander and get him to enact an AI, accuracy of information. It's a process in which we start a case to investigate further. They can get details much faster than you and I. They can find out who this Rana is; she's on the video. They'll contact her and get the details of where this girl is," he said reassuringly. "But it will take time, Jill; it's procedure." He punched several buttons on his phone before he hit send.

The words muffled as Jill's thoughts poked at her gut. Why was David so nonchalant about this girl? Something here, too, was amiss. How did she not know this about David? Did he not care about kids? Surely he couldn't be that obtuse about the fact that someone unauthorized had taken Gabriella. Unless. Unless... unless he knew something he was not telling her.

CHAPTER
THIRTY-NINE

The sharp jabs to the keyboard would have given Jerry Lee Lewis a run for his Great Balls of Fire piano finger punches. The clouds that covered the sun made the room feel dreary.

"Procedures, goddamn procedures!" Jill barked into the air as she wrote an email to Kali. Jill knew she could count on Kali to help. She was not officially working with Jill at the moment, but Jill could always rely on her research expertise. And if Jill were lucky, Kali would sneak in a few searches above her security clearance level, compliments of her new boy toy, Bob. "Gabriella Smith," Jill spoke aloud as she wrote. She added all the details and attached the snapshot she had taken. She included a note asking Kali to cross-reference the number with the girl's details and hit send.

Why was the girl repeating the number? She had Googled that number already to no avail. Now all she could do was wait. Wait. "Argh!" She slapped her laptop closed and leaned back. A slight mist hung in the air from too much humidity in the room. She could hear the sounds of honking horns below her window as her mind drifted. Why did it seem like David didn't care about Gabriella?

She thought about that number. Why would a child repeat a number like that? Was it an address? Jill had memorized it too: 1376833626. Ten digits. What did it mean? Jill vented her frustration with a big exaggerated sigh. The thought of David interrupted her release, and she checked the emotional pulse of her heart. She loved David. Her heart wobbled. His warm touch made her tingle as if transmitting a private signal to her soul. And then there was how he looked at her. His smile. That twinkle that only she could see when he looked at her, and sometimes he'd wink an I love you. She could see his tight quads pushing against the fabric, even with his army fatigues. She thought of his abs. She thought of his eyes. His persistent lovemaking. Jill blushed, and for a moment, she considered picking up the phone and telling him she needed him, and she needed him

now.Darkness battled hard. Allan. Leila. Stan Brown. How could her intuition be so jumbled? Her heart fought back with reason. After all, he was her husband. She had felt his sincerity, kindness, and love these past few days. But she felt something else too. Something sinister was whirling around her heart as she considered him.

Jill rose and walked toward the minibar. Well, what could she do about any of it right now? David was busy with another project that night. Busy. What could be more important than finding a lost little girl? What could be more important than finding his way back to Jill's heart? Jill sighed as she cracked open a bottle of water. As she reached for a glass, she accidentally kicked over her bag. The side of the little pouch slid out just enough for Jill to pause and notice. She set down the water, bent over, and picked up the pouch.

Jill sat on the bed, untied the leather cord that bound the worn leather case, and opened it. Clay numbers clinked as they tumbled onto the sheets. Ever since Matthew McGregor, Jill felt she could no longer Remote View. But when David went missing and Zayed was perceived dead, she felt she had no choice—she was desperate. Jill pushed past her fears in Hamburg and Dubai, and she was successful. She managed on her own, or so she thought, to track David around the Middle East, into Hamburg, Germany, and then the ultimate capture of Stan Brown in Abu Dhabi, United Arab Emirates. But her last Remote View was full of terror. It was like watching a horror movie. Zayed was beaten and then set on fire, alive. In that particular Remote View, David was there. He was in the shadows, and Jill had thought he was next to be roasted alive. But he wasn't killed; he was still alive. Jill pondered, moving the numbers around and around and around. She thought of Gabriella, the brothel, and the horrors it held. She wondered if she had the strength to Remote View again. She attempted several times after the arrest of Stan Brown and her last reliable Remote View. But it was no use. She had lost her Remote View mojo. Again.

But now, with virtually no help from David or anyone, for that matter, she'd have to do something. She'd have to risk seeing Matthew in her RV session. She could do it. She'd do it for Gabriella. Or maybe she should just wait. Wait for procedures, as David had attempted to appease her. "What do you have to lose? Why not try?" she said aloud. She picked up her notebook and pen, placed them beside the clay numbers, turned to a blank page, and wrote "location," then "brothel," and circled the words. She drew a line from the circle and wrote the word "target" along with a six-digit number ending in the digit one. The number was random; it was the digit one that was important. All Remote Views started this way.

In stage one of an RV session, the target was assigned a random number. "Optimum trajectory," the Remote Viewer guru had called it in Jill's training. "OT is the best place for your mind to be before we begin." To get there, the viewers were given target numbers. To achieve optimum trajectory, they started by placing their pens on the last digit—which was always the digit one. "Lose yourself in them; numb your thoughts." The process was sort of like a radio station signal drawing the viewer toward the target. All living things are made of energy, and it's been speculated that if a viewer can connect to the target on an energy level, the viewer can then see the target and its surroundings. In this stage, the viewer typically sits with a pen and paper to record the viewing. The viewer needs to be hyper-attentive and zero in on sights and sensations. In the FBI RV department, this was usually achieved through group meditation.

Somehow, though, Jill found that using the clay numbers served as a better tool than just writing. Maybe it was more for comfort or a ritual. All the Remote Viewers had a ritual. Jill's Grams always carried the pouch of Earth from the sacred mountains of their homeland, which was next to the Navajo reserve. She had told Jill many stories of the pouch's power. "All things are equal, and everything has a spirit," Grams would say. She was a singer, a healer, and she taught Jill that she, too, might have inherited her clairvoyance.

Jill huffed and mulled over the task before her. Record the sounds and smells. Then the tastes, textures, and feelings. Are you afraid, Jill? Mad or sad? What are the colors and textures? No thinking; just record what you see.

Jill propped up two pillows, reached over, and set her alarm. She didn't trust that she'd come back on time. She needed to be sure she would, especially if she was in bi-location, where she'd end up in two places simultaneously. Jill leaned back on the headboard and looked down at her notebook. She clicked on her pen and thought of Gabriella—thought of the brothel—and then took five long, deep yoga breaths and closed her eyes.

When I reach my realm of calm, I open my eyes. After a beat, holding my pen, I place the tip on the dot on the page next to the six-digit number. I look at my clay numbers and wait. Looking but not seeing, I need to feel it first. I need to feel the energy; plug me into the energy wave. Then it happens: my hand moves fast in one stroke from left to right. I look down at what looks like a drawing of a radio wave—just a simple squiggly line on the page. The ideogram. I know that every time my pen hits the page, now in the session, an electrical signal will enter the matrix of my mind. I trace the ideogram over and over and over. Something is happening. It is not supposed to happen this way.

My wide eyes stare into the darkness; I gasp. All I can see is blackness. The only sound I hear is sharp breaths snorting through my nose. I try to move my hands—my body. Nothing. I feel it. It is there. Fear. Am I having an out-of-body experience? Am I in bi-location? I do not know. I try to sit up—try to speak. Nothing. Frantic now, my breathing becomes a high-pitched squeal when a scream pierces the air from afar. I feel as if I have jumped out of my skin—out of my soul. Then I hear more. "No. Stop. No. eerrrrrrrrrrrhhhh."

A child, I think—a child in pain. My heart is beating fast now. I try to move, but the only thing I can move is my eyes. All I can see is blackness. I cannot panic. I will not panic. I will not panic. I breathe fast, snorts coming from my nose. And just when I think I will cross over the edge into the abyss of fear—into the abyss of hell—the sound of electricity bug-zaps above me. I look up to the right and blink, trying to focus on what I am seeing. Gold blurriness clears with every blink. I squeeze my eyes tight when I smell burning flesh. Then, without thought, I push past my fear, open my eyes wide, and blink at the large gold word "Hitler." My ears begin to ring. Ring. Ring. Ring.

Jill sat up fast, trying to catch her breath, and punched off the alarm on the side table. She huffed and coughed. Her lungs ached as if she were being smothered.

She looked down at the blank page with only the target written and the six-digit number. The child-like scribbles of the ideogram she had drawn had a pointy, star-like quality.

Disoriented, Jill reached to the right, snatched up her pen and pad, and began to write.

A: Shapes: Blackness. Sign that read "Hitler."

B: Man-made

C: Burning flesh. Breathing. A child screaming, maybe a girl or a boy? Electricity. A bell ringing.

Jill was shaking, and what she wrote was scribed with jagged lettering. She tried to review her notes, but she was nauseous now. She closed her eyes and did another five yoga breaths before she felt some semblance of herself.

Jill sat up and looked at the page, thinking for a moment. Hitler—why the word Hitler? As in Nazi? She turned to her mind map page that she had begun, wrote the word Hitler, and underlined it twice—then started to mind map. Nazi. Dictator. Absolute ruler.

But that didn't feel right. After all, she was concentrating on a location—the location of the brothel. She again wrote the phrase "location of brothel" and circled it. What does Hitler, or Germany for that matter, have to do with the brothel's location in Istanbul?

Jill stood on wobbly legs. This was common after a Remote View, as the amount of energy used to surf the eight-lane dimension was intense and took a toll on her physical psyche. She walked over to the computer and sat down. She tapped the words "Istanbul and Hitler" into Google search, with brackets included. A map of Istanbul was the first term in the index. The red marker blinked on the screen. Zooming in, she saw the word Oschitler SK—a street in Istanbul. This made sense to Jill. She was looking for a location—the location of the brothel. It must be correct. Excited, Jill wrote Oschitler and underlined the spelling of Hitler in the name. She was onto something. She knew she was.

Jill moused over Google Maps, changed the view to satellite, and zoomed in along the street. She clicked on street view and moved virtually along the road. What was Jill looking at? What was she looking for? There were blocks and blocks and blocks of villas. Who was she kidding? She needed help. She'd knock on David's door and just suck it up, taking his jabs about being a psychic queen. She needed to get David and find a way to get to the brothel. Someone must know where it was. The recollection of the smell of burning flesh kicked Jill into action, and she headed for the door.

CHAPTER FORTY

Jill knocked on David's door. No answer. Perhaps he was downstairs. Jill returned to her room and grabbed her phone before closing the door. She needed to tell David about her Remote View. Hell, they could figure out their relationship later. Gabriella needed her. She knew she did. She needed to tell him about the street called Oschitler. She had to get there. She had to save Gabriella. Panic began to bubble in her gut as she walked into the residence lobby.

She scanned the room. At nine o'clock, a different man sat behind the makeshift concierge desk that backed onto a large glass wall. At three o'clock was the security station and exit. And in between was the cafeteria and lobby combined. It was empty. Why hadn't she taken David's number today? She knew there were no contacts on her phone. It was then a thought tapped her brain. She studied the phone and wondered if maybe it was her phone that was giving away their location all along. This thought quickly left when she felt the man behind the desk staring at her.

She walked over and stood directly before him. "Can I help you, Miss Oliver?"

"I know this is not a real hotel or anything, but I need some assistance," Jill said. The man nodded. "Has David Brown left a message for me?"

The man looked at the screen that illuminated before him, then looked back at Jill blankly. "No, Miss Oliver. We have no message for you."

"No messages for me?" He shook his head. "What do you mean no messages for me? Does that mean you have a message from David for someone else?"

The man looked back at the screen and politely nodded. "No, there are no messages from David Brown to anyone else."

"But..."

The man frowned. "I'm not at liberty to discuss other guests' messages, Miss Oliver."

Jill thought about his answer. If there weren't any incoming messages from David, why would he word his response in such a way? David must have a message, then. But from whom?

"Excuse me, Miss Oliver, is there anything else I can help you with?" Jill shook her head. The phone blared, interrupting the man's stare, and he moved slightly to the left, writing something down. His movement was just slight enough for Jill to see the glare of his computer screen reflect off the pane of glass. She studied the words, ingraining them backward before turning them around: DAVID BROWN: I found what you are looking for.

She pulled out her phone and dialed Yildiz 008222262.

CHAPTER FORTY-ONE

Jill sat at the small wooden table in the lobby cafeteria—the same table where she had seen David earlier. She watched Yildiz approach. Dressed in black, the same as before, Jill pondered whether this attire was mandatory for her Muslim faith. She remembered wearing the black abaya and how hot and uncomfortable it had been when she was disguised in Doha and Abu Dhabi. Yildiz wasn't dressed in the thick polyester black robe that Muslim women wore in that part of the Middle East.

"Thank you for coming," Jill gestured for Yildiz to sit down. "As I said on the phone, David told me you were the local Turkey expert here who works for the CIA. Well, I can't seem to find David right now, and I have something pressing I need help with."

Yildiz nodded and sat across from the table. "Yes, but I don't work for the CIA. I'm independent."

"Yeah, he mentioned that too."

"You said you'd explain how you got my number when we met. I am here now," she said in perfect English.

Jill nodded and took a drink of water from her bottle.

"Did David give you my number?"

"Not exactly." Jill looked over at the empty reception desk. Yildiz followed her gaze.

"Ah, I see," Yildiz said, studying Jill. "You should not read someone else's messages."

Jill gave a half-smile. "Yeah, I'm sorry about that, but as I said, I can't reach David, and I need help from someone who knows Istanbul. What did you find for David?"

Yildiz stared at Jill and didn't say anything.

"Fine. I don't really care. Anyway, David told me you were from here. He stated that they hired you for HUMINT." Yildiz's right eyebrow lifted as she continued to listen. Jill pushed the lone notepad stationery page across the table to Yildiz.

"Oschitler." Yildiz's eyes widened. "What is it you are looking for, Jill?"

Jill's eyes softened. "How do I say your name? Is it Yil, diz?" Jill sounded it out, and Yildiz nodded. "I know this is going to sound far-fetched, but I need help finding someone."

"Go on."

"Actually, I need help finding a twelve-year-old girl."

A puzzled look grew on Yildiz's face, and she said, "A girl? Whatever for?"

"I know you don't know me, or I you, for that matter, but the agency has vetted you. Well, David has. And I don't have any choice right now..." Jill trailed off. She thought about how much she should tell this woman. She was a stranger to Jill. The smell of burning flesh pushed her forward. "Like I said, I can't reach David."

Yildiz sucked in a sharp, subtle breath. "You mentioned this, yes."

"And I know you haven't heard from him, as he hasn't picked up your message either."

"Please tell me where you think this girl is and where you got this street name. Oschitler?"

Jill wondered how to answer this question. She knew Yildiz was a Turk, and she wore a hijab, which meant she was not only of the Muslim faith but also a devoted Muslim. David used the term psychic magic, and Jill knew discussing any psychic or magic in this faith was not good. Haram, she remembered. To attempt to explain anything about Remote Viewing would only prove to be futile, Jill thought. So she replied with the next best answer. "Google, I guess."

"Alright," Yildiz sidestepped over to her next question. "Why do you think this girl can be found on this street?"

Jill had to think fast. "I read somewhere that there were brothels in this part of Istanbul, and I thought it would be the best place to begin searching. I mean, there can't be that many around."

"A brothel?"

Jill nodded, and Yildiz didn't ask further. She just spoke as if thinking out loud. "A twelve-year-old girl in a brothel. What is her nationality?"

"What difference does that make?"

"Jill, this is Turkey, and this street you speak of is in our red-light district. There are many brothels there. Many girls are there from many different countries." Her tongue curled when she hit the letter r. "As sad as this sounds, prostitution is an industry here; it's a booming business. Such places are overlooked because they pay to be ignored. My dear Jill, it appears you do not know much about my home country. Have you ever heard of the enforced disappearance act?" Yildiz continued. "It's a UN protection instrument. It's meant to protect the citizens of Turkey from disappearing—crimes against humanity and all that. We've had a dangerous history. We should not speak about the thousands of Kurds killed in our history. There is much crime here. A brothel here is a normal part of our way of life. It's not like the West." Jill blinked, wondering if she just heard what she thought she had.

Yildiz pressed on. "So if you know her nationality, this will narrow the search. Girls are sold into categories."

"Categories?"

Yildiz nodded.

"She's American, or so she said when she went to the American Embassy." Jill filled in the blanks.

"American Embassy?" Yildiz studied Jill, looking for a response that made sense. "Why is she not there now? An American girl as a sex slave is very rare." Jill explained what happened at the Embassy. "Ah, I understand now. One moment." Yildiz held up a finger before pulling out her phone and dialing a series of numbers.

Jill sat watching Yildiz and listened. She did not know or understand Turkish, so profiling was all she had to discover any clues. Yildiz was a calm, soft-spoken speaker. She almost had a robotic tone. Several moments and calls later, Yildiz clunked her phone down onto the table. "I think I know which brothel this girl is in."

Jill's lips flatlined. "What? How?"

"Like I said, it's a big industry here. Accepted. I know people who know where these types of white girls are kept. They are more valuable than the Kurds or South Asian girls. They bring in a better dollar."

"When can we go?" Jill rose quickly.

"We?" Yildiz said, standing in front of Jill. "It is not safe for you, Jill. I'm aware you are some sort of analyst and..."

Jill scowled at Yildiz, but Yildiz continued. "This district in Turkey is not safe for someone such as yourself."

"I'm going, Yildiz! Just tell me where this place is, and I will go there myself," Jill said stubbornly.

Yildiz studied Jill. "Fine then. I have called a driver. You will need to be prepared for what you will see. You will need to be careful of what may happen. We cannot just walk in and take the girl. That would be too dangerous. You must agree to my instructions. Otherwise, I will not jeopardize myself for your cause."

Jill looked at her harshly. Who did this woman think she was? Who did she think Jill was? But she had no choice, so she nodded.

"Come on, then, let us go." Jill followed Yildiz out the door.

CHAPTER FORTY-TWO

The minibus smelled of orange air freshener that attempted to mask the scent of stale cigarette smoke. As Yildiz had instructed, there was no talking on the twenty-minute trip to Ocshitler Street. Rows of concrete villas lined the busy road, making it hard to differentiate one block from the next. With so many turns, Jill's situational awareness was strained.

The driver pulled up in front of a crowded alleyway and stopped where Yildiz had instructed. She nodded to Jill to depart from the small minibus. The door slid shut before either of them spoke.

Jill looked down the alleyway that hugged a hodgepodge of night shoppers. It seemed like a marketplace. People gathered around a man yelling about what Jill believed to be the day's fresh fish. "It doesn't look like brothels would be here," she said as she began to walk through the crowded cobblestone alley.

"We could not stop in front of where I suspect this girl is," Yildiz said pointedly. "They have people watching these places—they pay for protection."

"What's our plan?" Jill queried. "I have no weapon. I had to hand over my Sig Sauer at the Embassy. And that little twerp in the security booth would not give it back without special clearance."

Yildiz nodded blankly. It was evident to Jill that Yildiz was concentrating or calculating, maybe. She didn't know for sure. One thing she
did know for certain was that she needed to watch her own back. Jill
began her scans as they pushed past people, but too many things were
happening to profile to any degree.

Yildiz stopped at the dead end of the alley and peered around the
end of the building. Jill followed. Yildiz looked at a dingy yellow
villa about one hundred yards away. It had a ten-foot concrete wall
surrounding it. The large black steel gates in the front were rusted,
with speckles of brown pushing through chipped paint. The doors
were wide enough to fit a car through. A single door stood beside the
gate. In between them, mounted on the wall, was an intercom with a
plaque inscribed in Turk Mägo.

"Please, Jill," Yildiz commanded. "Please stay here, and I will go in
and see if someone will talk to me about this

girl.""But ..." Jill looked Yildiz straight in the eye, but Yildiz was
looking over Jill's shoulder. Jill turned and looked down the alley. Two
women were shouting at each other a few feet away, trying to buy the
same piece of jewelry. "What?"

"It is nothing," Yildiz hushed. "We must be very careful. Please.
Please stand here and watch the alley and watch the house. Do not
move."

This pissed Jill off. Hell no, she wasn't going to be a lookout. Not
here—not now. "I'm coming with you," Jill insisted.

Yildiz squared her shoulders and stood directly in front of Jill. "You
will need to be smart about this. If I go, a Muslim woman, they will
let me in. I will pose as a buyer." Yildiz stated this matter-of-factly. "It
would make sense to them. Women are part of the corrupt side of this
industry. If I bring a white American female, they will not trust me. I
will get more answers for you going in alone."

Jill didn't like anyone telling her what to do. But she'd have to agree; it made more sense. Jill wore black fatigues, and her law enforcement boots were certainly not inconspicuous. "What will you do, ring the doorbell and ask if an American child is being held against her will?" Jill huffed out, resigned to not going to the brothel.

"That is exactly what I will do. Everything here is negotiable. I'm not the police, nor would they care if I was. Most of the police are paid to leave them alone," Yildiz said. "Be careful," and she started walking along a dirt path toward the villa.

Jill leaned against the cold wall, watched as Yildiz stood before the smaller steel door, and pressed the intercom button. She couldn't hear from this distance. Jill couldn't understand what they were saying anyway. Yildiz nodded as she talked through the small box. The door slowly opened, and a plump woman stuck her head out and looked around. It appeared that she was looking straight in Jill's direction. Jill slowly turned her head, looking back down the alley, and turned around just in time to watch Yildiz enter.

Several minutes passed. As Jill waited, she thought again about David and wondered where he was. She wondered if he would be concerned if Jill was not at the embassy residence. The thought passed as Jill did her scans again, then looked back at the entrance to the villa. No movement. Several lights turned on in two separate rooms, but the window coverings were solid, and only a sliver of light peeked out.

Jill pulled out her phone and turned it on. The screen lit up. No messages and no missed calls. "Damn it," she said out loud. But who would call her anyway on this phone?

"Can I help you?"

Jill's hands flew up in fright as she turned quickly and faced two men. They were dressed in uniform. The baby-blue shirts were neatly pressed. Their black pants were held up by police belts that sported the longest billy club Jill had ever seen. "Police," the taller of the two men said. "Can we be of assistance? Are you lost?" Jill studied them and thought about what Yildiz had said about the police in Istanbul.

"Eh ... ch, I'm... I'm just looking for some souvenirs." Jill nodded at the table that was at least ten feet away. The officers looked over at the table full of shishas and tobacco, then back to Jill. "I ... uh, thought I heard my mobile." Jill looked at the blank-faced stares. "I'm on my way back to my hotel. I'm not lost. Thank you," Jill said in an attempt to maintain her façade. She pushed past the two officers and headed back into the alley. Jill didn't look back at them, but she could feel their stares burning a hole in her tight ass as she blended into the shopping crowd. She was halfway down before she stopped and appeared to be looking at Turkish mosaic lamps. Jill slowly glanced in her peripheral vision. She could not see them. Sure, it could have been that the packed crowds were covering them up. She waited and repeated the motion. They were gone.

Jill paced her way back, as a shopper would, carefully stopping at several more tables stacked with vibrant goods that lined the alley. She did not see the two police officers and wondered if they were watching the villa or had gone over to the villa and somehow summoned help. She reached the corner where they had confronted her and slowly looked past the concrete corner of the wall towards the villa.

The front gates of the villa were dark now—the street was silent. Screw it! Jill moved into the shadows towards the villa. She was cautious, scanning in all four directions. She was careful enough until she heard it. A scream. Was it a woman? A child?

Instinct made her run. She ran fast towards the gates. The large steel door was not locked. Jill yanked the handle down, pulled hard on the door, opened it, and entered. Inside, the courtyard was all concrete. Concrete everywhere. Two brown wooden doors adorned the front entrance and were wide open. Jill moved quickly as she heard another scream. A little too soon. Too quick to see the man who must have burst through the open front door seconds before her. The sound of the gun being racked made Jill freeze. He said something to her in a different language she did not understand. Jill slowly raised her arms in surrender and turned around. A heavy-set man with a bald head that looked like he'd been in a fight with a bulldog had his back against the wall. He was holding a 9mm Luger at waist level and looked amused when he saw Jill's face.

It only took a second for Jill to calculate the distance. She was close enough. She lunged forward and walloped his arm sideways, moving the barrel out of her direction. With one fast kick to the groin, the man doubled over. Jill jumped up and, using all her weight, smashed her elbow down hard into the back of his neck. His teeth scattered as his jaw hit the floor.

Instinctively, Jill picked up the gun, pushed the button, released the magazine, and checked it. Nine bullets. That meant one was in the chamber. Jill heard women shouting, and one sounded hysterical. She didn't have time to check her surroundings. She didn't have a chance to check on the man who was not moving. Jill ran toward an opening ten feet down the hall. She stopped short inside the brightly lit room.

Yildiz stood in a fighting stance in front of the pudgy woman holding a gun to a teenage girl's head. The girl was distraught, yelling and crying. Snot streamed down her lips as she spat something in a different language. But Jill knew body language; the girl was pleading. And by the look on the pudgy woman's face, the girl was begging for her life. It only took a second for Jill to comprehend what was happening. But what happened next occurred too fast. Pain seared as Jill's body lurched forward from a kick to her back. She fell and slid on the marble floor, letting out a grunt. Yildiz turned toward her. Jill scrambled to her feet. Without forethought, Jill and Yildiz immediately had their backs to each other, moving in unison, turning. Jill watched the man she thought she had knocked out stumble toward her. Jill held out her arms and aimed the gun at his chest.

The pudgy woman yelled something at him, including the word "gun." But before Jill could instinctively pull the trigger, the man's eyes fluttered and rolled back in his head. He spat blood when his chin hit the hard marble four feet in front of her.

The girl whimpered. "Noooooooooooo." Jill turned as Yildiz lunged forward toward the pair. But Yildiz was not fast enough. She was not close enough. Blood spattered against the wall as a bullet passed through the girl's skull. The girl crumpled to the right as the plump woman pointed the gun in Yildiz's direction. Jill raised the gun to shoot the woman, but Yildiz jumped directly in Jill's aim and bashed the woman's arm upwards. The woman's gun fired, and the bullet hit the roof, raining concrete pebbles. Yildiz let out a guttural scream and moved like a ninja. Her knife sliced the woman's jugular in one swift move. Blood sprayed the room, and the woman dropped the gun. She was frantically grabbing at her throat. The woman turned, and blood sprayed the dingy yellow walls before she fell to the ground. Seconds passed, and the fountain of life drained onto the concrete floor.

"Why'd you do that!" Jill yelled to Yildiz as Yildiz wiped her blade on the dead woman's skirt. Jill was breathing heavily. "Why, Yildiz? We needed her alive! I could have shot the gun out of her hand."

Yildiz stood with great calmness and spoke. "You were not fast enough."

Jill was frantic now, and with exasperation, she said, "This is not Gabriella. There must be more of them—more girls."

Calmly, as if guiding children across a busy street, Yildiz held her hand up, gesturing up the stairs. "There is no one else here."

"What! What do you mean?" Jill looked back at the girl on the floor. She didn't look much older than sixteen.

"Her name was Elsa; she would have talked. I asked her about this American girl. She said the girls had been moved. Sold. Then that fat bitch grabbed Elsa before I could stop her. I assessed the situation in error. She was fast. Too fast." Yildiz looked down at the bloody woman as if calculating her mistake. Then she looked back up at Jill. "I would have apprehended that woman if you had not entered the room." There was a slight twitch in Yildiz's right eye but nothing else. Then she said evenly, "Now we will not know who they were sold to." Yildiz turned fast. "Come with me now. We must leave. I have an idea. Let us go. Hurry!"

CHAPTER
FORTY-THREE

"I don't understand, Yildiz. I mean, where would they go? Who would buy them?" Jill questioned as they briskly walked toward the spot where the driver was instructed to wait. "You must find out who has bought them."

Yildiz stopped abruptly and looked squarely at Jill. "This is a business decision. Someone needed girls—young girls—and a lot of them. This brothel will find more girls—new girls. And the same thing will happen again. The girl Elsa began to tell me about a large shipment when that woman came without notice and grabbed the girl."

They began walking again. "I thought you were an administrator or something," Yildiz said as they approached the white minibus. "You are trained." Yildiz nodded to the driver, and he nodded back.

"I, uh... I'm not exactly an administrator. Did David tell you that?" Yildiz gave her a blank look. "I'm a terrorist profiler, to be more accurate. I'm here on assignment." Jill thought about how much to tell Yildiz.

"I did not know profilers were trained in hand-to-hand."

"Muay Thai," Jill added. "It's more of a hobby than something I need to use in my job. And what about you?"

"Krav Maga. Now we must go."

"Wait," Jill blurted, about to grab Yildiz's sleeve. But she stopped herself and said, "Can you find anything out about a shipment of girls?" Yildiz nodded as she opened the door and slid across the back seat.

It was a quiet ride back to the Embassy. Jill contemplated what had happened at the villa and how Yildiz seemed a little too eager to help her. I'm paranoid, Jill thought. Who wouldn't want to help a child? When they got out and closed the door, Yildiz spoke first. "Girls are traded all the time here. They were probably just sold to a neighboring city. Perhaps Maslak or Konya. I will ask my people. But I am afraid if it is a large group of girls, then it is probably organized by the Bubbas, the local mafia, and if it is them, no one will talk about it—no one. I will bill you for my services to help you. I am a professional. I will get David to approve the payment." Jill gave Yildiz her mobile number before returning to the minibus and driving away.

Inside the residence, Jill approached the concierge. "Messages?" The man said nothing. He just pressed a button. The sound of the dot matrix printer tapped ink frantically onto paper. The man ripped the paper off the printer, folded the holed edges, ripped them off, and handed the paper to Jill.

Jill started to read it but was interrupted. "Miss Oliver. Jill Oliver." Jill looked up and saw two large men approaching. The security guards looked like sumo wrestlers as they stood before her.

"Yes?"

"You are required to come with us."

"What? Go with you? Where?" Jill protested. "I'm not going any where..."

One of the men grabbed her elbow while the other spoke. "It's not an option, ma'am. The Commander wants to see you, and right now."

"Stop," Jill said forcefully, trying to pull her elbow free.

He held his grip tight, moving her through the security doors and into the Embassy.

CHAPTER
FORTY-FOUR

They sat in the same meeting room as the day before, but the lights seemed brighter.

"Coffee?" Todd, the assistant to the Commander, said to Jill.

"What's this about?" Jill demanded.

Todd stood with his back to her while pouring the coffee. "Did you want a coffee, Miss Oliver?" he asked again.

"No," Jill said, annoyed.

Ian, the Commander, sat across from her. "Just some routine questions regarding the death of Allan Mars and what happened in the truck."

"Routine? You call having two goons grab me in that lobby routine?"

No one refuted it.

"If it is so routine, can it not wait until morning?" Jill spouted. She was relieved and glad they hadn't grabbed her because of what happened at the brothel. Besides, how would they find out that quickly anyway? "Fine, but let's make it fast, okay? I've got things to do besides sitting in this room," Jill conceded.

She began to read the message the concierge had handed her. "It's from us," Todd said before she could finish reading it. "We left it earlier since you did not answer your phone. We had also asked you to stay inside the Embassy residence. You were warned that it is not safe outside our jurisdiction. I know we can't stop you without reasonable grounds."

"Reasonable grounds? Reasonable grounds for what?" Jill pulled out her phone and swiped the screen. Three missed calls. It must have been on silent mode. One call was from 090 23132, and the other two were from an unknown +0 number. David? She didn't have time for this CIA bullshit right now. She needed to call David. But how? How could she call an unknown +0 number? Jill thumbed the screen looking for any text messages. But there were none.

"Jill... Jill," Ian interrupted her thoughts. "This won't take long, I promise. Please put the phone away," he said pointedly.

Jill placed the phone on the table, face up. "You said reasonable grounds. What the hell are you talking about?"

Todd sat down and gulped coffee. "Tell us about what happened with Allan Mars. We just want to have a better understanding. Reasonable grounds is a term we use; please do not read into it. But you must know, we cannot be responsible for you if you do not follow what is suggested you do here." Jill glared at them and paused, crossing her arms. Annoyance seethed in her words as she described in detail a repeat of what had transpired, leaving out the head-smashing lie. She took a moment, grabbed a bottle of water off the table, cracked it open, and wondered if she should tell them about the rabbit punch. She was visualizing how hard David hit Allan when Ian asked a strange question. "How long have you known David—your husband, David Brown?"

The question caught Jill off guard. But before she could ask—before she could answer and before she could say what the hell was going on—Ian said, "We know you've only been married for just over a year now. That's public knowledge. But how well do you know him, Jill? Would you say you have a good marriage?"

Jill felt befuddled. This sounded like something other than a routine question. It was not routine at all, she surmised. "Of course, we have a good marriage," Jill said.

Ian leaned back. "That's good, Jill. That's good to hear."

Jill squinted and said, "Is that it? Can I go now?" No one answered. Todd leaned forward and looked Jill squarely in the eyes as if analyzing hers. She recognized what he was doing. He was getting ready to gauge her response to his next question. Then it came.

"We know you know Leila Sorel." Jill was confused and tried to understand. A stitch pulled in her gut. Then he asked, "How well do you know her?"

CHAPTER FORTY-FIVE

"Leila Sorel?" Jill was perplexed. "Of course, I know Leila..." Then she thought about it. She wondered how well she really did know her. Surely her query to Eric was just her paranoia. What she wrote in her notebook crept back into Jill's thoughts. The nagging thought, too, bounced into her mind. The phone call at David's closed office door. The one he lied about. The one Leila had confessed to. Jill's gut began to bubble, with little pinpricks bursting with each one.

"I ... I eh," Jill stuttered. "Why are you asking me about Leila Sorel? She's not in Turkey, is she?" The two men glanced sideways at each other and then back to Jill. "Well, is she here? Why the hell are you asking me about her?"

Todd stared blankly at her. Jill couldn't read him. She was a goddamn profiler, and she couldn't read this poker-faced man. Was he nervous or just happy watching Jill squirm? "Look," Jill sidestepped. "Have you heard from David today?" Another sideways glance between dumb and dumber.

Ian spoke. "This isn't an interrogation, Miss Oliver," he said like a cat tapping a toy mouse with its paw. "We just have new intel about Miss Sorel."

"Intel?"

"Well..." Todd leaned back and watched Jill. She knew she was being examined. "It's not anything we can disclose to you. Jill, again, Leila Sorel, tell us how you know her. How did you meet her? How well do you know her?"

Jill crossed her arms, taking the Fifth.

"Look, Miss Oliver," he said pointedly, "this may be a question of national security, and you do know the penalty for obstructing an investigation."

"Investigation? What investigation? You said you had routine questions. Now you are telling me that it's a matter of national security. I know about national security. It's my job!" Jill's chair burped across the floor as she stood fast.

Both men stood in unison. "Miss Oliver," Ian said, "this is a serious matter. Please. Please sit down." He gestured his hand towards her chair.

Begrudgingly, Jill sat down. A serious matter—what the hell? Jill thought to herself. She was supposedly on a fake assignment in Turkey with the ever-disappearing David, aka her untrustworthy husband. She was attacked in a brothel while looking for a kidnapped child and was now apparently a sold child. A child that somehow managed to disappear from the refuge of the American Embassy. And now these twerps were asking her about Leila and national security? Leila. Leila! Her thoughts stopped sputtering around in her head; where the hell was David?

CHAPTER FORTY-SIX

Somewhere in Istanbul, Turkey

"Where did you get it?" Laudman232 held out his large hand and looked at the mobile storage device.

The small man squirmed in the front seat of the old, tattered Corolla, placed it gently into his palm, and stuttered. "The—the—the rock." He balled his hands and flexed his fingers as if shaking off an assumed taboo residue from the device.

Laudman232 was always amazed at how easy it was to conceal the Bluetooth device under a rock. All it took was a pause for the upload, a quick cigarette or something, and the intel was transmitted before being deleted. It was the new age of geocaching. Back in the day, before technology, you'd need a marker, a sign or something, and a shovel to dig up the military geocache full of intel.

"Were you followed?" Laudman232 asked. The small man shook his head. He was a mule, a modern-day delivery boy. Laudman232 handed him a roll of cash, and the small man stepped out of the car, jumped onto his moped, kicked on the start, and skittered away.

Laudman232 thumbed the mobile device, clicked several buttons, and read the screen. Scorpion? "Scorpion," he said with a hushed breath. He was dressed in loose-fitting army fatigues, placed the device in his left leg-side pocket, looked at his watch, and started the car. Dust flew as gravel spat backward, and he pulled onto the empty lane. Beads of sweat formed as he thought about what he had just read. He knew he didn't have much time. He'd never seen the command before but knew what it meant. Scorpion was the code word for assassination.

Eight minutes later, he found what he was looking for and parked. Laudman232 peered out the rear-view mirror and did surveillance on his surroundings. The only person on the dark cobblestone street was a man struggling to pull an old wooden cart on wooden wheels. The building he was looking for was tall and thin and held a large green sign that blinked "Internet Cafe."

Laudman232 darted toward the cement building on the quiet street. Shadows cast spells from dark doorways as he walked past. Inside the dingy shop was a narrow staircase. It creaked as he climbed the stairs. On the first floor, four computers hummed and displayed a dancing screensaver of cartoon belly dancers. An Asian man was the only other occupant in the room. He was smoking so much that it looked like he had two cigarettes in both corners of his mouth.

Laudman232 sat at the computer in the corner, logged into Hotmail, and fumbled the mouse as he tried to click on the drafts folder. There were no new saved draft messages. A drop of sweat plopped onto the keyboard as he stared at the empty folder. There should have been a reply by now, at least some sort of response. Something was wrong.

The password had stayed the same. A changed password was their code to say that there was a breach. He was halfway around the world in a different time zone, but this was how they communicated: write a draft message and save it. Check the draft folder for a response, then delete the message. Nothing was ever sent over the unsafe World Wide Web. Nothing was ever transmitted. But with the new knowledge of the command, Scorpion, he knew he had to act now.

Laudman232 looked around the room again. The Asian man was busy tapping on the keyboard as smoke puffed from his nose. A younger man appeared behind the entrance desk and was playing a video game. Laudman232 looked back at his screen, then clicked open a Gmail account on a different private Internet browser and began writing a new email message.

Problem shipment. No message from the buyer. Scorpion. Still implement?

Laudman232 clicked on "save as draft" and logged out. It was earlier in the recipient's time zone, and he figured he would get the message in about two hours. He would return here or find another Internet café in a few hours.

He stood and walked to the window to survey the street before leaving. He was careful not to attract the attention of the Asian man, who was busy lighting another cigarette. He leaned his forehead against the glass and peered down the street toward his parked car. He stiffened as he saw two men jump from a black SUV, slam their doors, and hurriedly walk toward his vehicle. Sweat began to seep from his armpits. He whirled, headed to the door, and down the rickety stairs, taking two at a time. He didn't have a chance to think, but he knew he had to get away from his car. He slowly opened the door, holding the bell that hung above it so it would not ring, and peered out. To his right, clothing hung out to dry, swaying on a thin line strewn across the dirt street. It was dark now, and what was left of the glowing dusk bounced off the satellite dishes that checkered the dingy buildings.

He couldn't go back to his vehicle, so he continued in the opposite direction. Sweat dripped into his eyes from his sweaty bald head, stinging them. They'd be lurking around, waiting for him to show up. How did they find him? He jogged down a back street. Flipping open his phone as he strode, he dialed a series of numbers. He barked into the phone, "Whiskey. Alpha. Romeo. Papa." WARP; warp meant to go to an agreed-upon destination when extraction was urgent.

He nodded and looked around for a landmark. Above him was a bright blue sign: Istiklal Street. He spoke, repeating the word "India. Sierra. Tango. India. Kilo. Lima. Alpha. Lima." He nodded and said, "WILCO," which meant I have understood and will comply with your instructions. He walked to the corner of the street, stepping back into the shadows, and waited. Minutes passed, and a black SUV drove up fast. A cloud of dust puffed over it as he jumped in, closed the door, and before he could say anything, the truck spat gravel and sped away.

"It wasn't the spooks; they were dressed like ... like ..." Laudman232 bellowed as sweat dribbled down his forehead. "I think it was the Gladios."

"How do you know it was the Gladios?" the driver asked in a broad American accent.

"Of course, it's the Gladios ... but how did they know where to find me?"

"The Gladios are everywhere, my friend." The driver blew a puff of cigar smoke that stifled his sentence.

"What do they want with me? We've made all the payments. They're paid well to protect us." Silence hung heavy as Laudman232 contemplated what was happening. "Something has changed." His body shifted as they made a hard right. "What..." Then a thought smacked him on the side of his head. "Wait. I got a message today. It was one word." Laudman232 fumbled through his pockets nervously. "Scorpion." He tried to find the mobile device with the message. The driver sped up fast and popped onto a bridge that took them into Tarlabaşı, a dangerous district of Istanbul that even the police wouldn't enter. Laudman232 looked around. "Where are we going?"

The driver gruffed under his breath something inaudible. He pulled a .45 Colt 1911 from his chest holster and fired a single shot into the man's head. Brain matter splattered against the passenger window as Laudman232's body slumped forward. David Brown said, puffing a smoky breath, "Because he knows what you have done."

The SUV turned a sharp left and pulled into a long-abandoned alley. David reached over the dead man and cranked on the handle before lifting his boot and kicking the body covered in shards of bone and blood out the door.

CHAPTER
FORTY-SEVEN

Jill seethed as she entered her room. She sat on the bed, unlaced her boots, and kicked them off. "What the hell is going on now?" Jill grumbled out loud. "They think I don't know my friggin' husband. How well do I know David?" This statement stung her, and that surprised her. It was the very thought she'd been contemplating since she saw David in Tucson several days ago. Sure, she rolled over this question over and over and over. But to have strangers ask her the same question—it was all too personal; it was all too much.

She had stopped at David's door on her way to her room and knocked—again, no answer. She thought about Ian and Todd and how they hadn't responded to the question of when they last saw David. And why Leila? Why now? Why here in Turkey? There was no response from them and no response from David either. Well, maybe he was the one who had called her. Jill didn't recall a discussion of exchanging phone numbers. She didn't even know how to reach him now. How well do I know my husband? Stupid. Of course, she knew David. But really, why hadn't she asked him for his new mobile number? This thought troubled her. The pressure of the day's events began to crack her resolve.

Did they think she was involved in Allan's death? What the heck was that all about? A stone dropped in her gut, so heavy she almost stumbled. And the question about Leila. Jill's heart darkened. And honestly, if she thought carefully about their questions, she had to ask herself—what did she really know about Leila? Jill sat, leaned back, put her feet on the desk, and contemplated the question. "Leila. Leila Sorel," she hushed and closed her eyes, willing herself into the tunnels.

She'd known Leila almost as long as she had known David. Well, not really "known" her, she thought. Just because you like someone doesn't mean you know them. She was already married to David for several months before she met Leila. And it was an odd introduction, an impromptu meeting, accidental, really. It was one of those rare cool nights they were out for dinner. It was a beautiful evening at a local Mexican haunt in Tucson. Three Mexican men were serenading them with Mexican guitars. They looked as if they were straight from the stage of an old Western theater show.

Jill began to hum the romantic ballad "Un Amor" by the Gypsy Kings as she continued flicking through the tunnels of her mind. As her thoughts deepened, she remembered the romance that crossed between her and David that night. Jill remembered how happy she was. And she remembered being left alone far too long at the table. She remembered finally getting up to check out where he was and why David had taken so long in the washroom. She remembered seeing him deep in discussion with a tall black woman—Leila. And then she remembered the look on David's face as Jill approached them. David's head tilted as he listened to Leila speak, and it suddenly straightened when he saw Jill. His whole demeanor stiffened. At the time, the awkward vibe did not strike Jill as anything of interest. And if she felt something was wrong, she had ignored it. The woman held out her hand and said, "Jill, I'm Leila. Happy to finally meet you." She had a firm handshake, and her face held some amusement.

Suddenly, Jill sat up, breaking her recollection, and grabbed her notebook. She turned to the pages Leila herself had written on in Hamburg and on the plane. It was a list of details, not in any particular order—a journalistic style. "Alright, Leila," Jill mused. "Let me see if I can follow your thought process." Jill turned to a blank page in the notebook and wrote the word "Leila," scratching two underlines beneath it. Then she wrote below: Who are you?

She began to write a list.

Photographer

NOC

Friend?

Friend of David's or

Work colleagues

The word "colleagues" caught Jill. She wrote the word "Brussels" and underlined it. Leila was a colleague of David's, but why was she looking for him so far away from the U.S.? And why was she in Brussels? She had met up with Stan Brown. Jill's gut pricked. Jill admitted to herself now that it was a bit of a coincidence. And it was a coincidence that both she and David's father ended up in Hamburg, where Jill had just landed hours before—another coincidence? Jill wrote the words "Leila" and "Stan" under the name "Brussels." She wrote the word "Hamburg" and the phrase "same time."

Hamburg. How could it even be possible that they were all in Hamburg at the same time? She recalled why she was there in the first place. The notebook. David's notebook. The one she found in Kushka. The one with her picture. Those words were not in David's handwriting. No one would have known she was going to Hamburg. She hadn't even had time to let Kali know. And the revelation that the only reason Jill went to Hamburg was that the clue in David's notebook was something only Jill knew herself at the time she found it. Then she wrote down the next thing that popped into her head. "David lied." She said it out loud as she wrote these two words. As she thought about this, she began to doodle. She was used to it, doodling in her Remote Viewing sessions. Ideograms and doodles were something she always did when deep in thought. She looked at Leila's name. She looked at Stan Brown's name next to "David lied." She spoke the words out loud. "Leila. Stan. David lied." Then, "Brussels. Hamburg." She said them in a chant-like manner. Minutes passed, and nothing significant came to her mind. Then she stopped and looked at the corner of the page where she had been doodling. She gasped as she looked at the star she had just drawn.

CHAPTER
FORTY-EIGHT

Jill sat back and blinked at the page. A star, another star. This star was different from the last star she had drawn. The previous star that she had drawn had six points. It was the Star of David, she surmised then. Jill flipped back in her notepad to the page where she drew the first star and studied it.

She recalled what Kali had said to her about it. Kali was very interested in the number of points and their position. She needed to call Kali. It was important—something about the number of points.

Why had she just drawn another star? Another star, but this one had only four points. Then there was the photo Leila had taken in Brussels. Jill thought she had kept the picture, and she tipped her notebook upside down, flipping the pages. Nothing fell out. Placing the notebook back down, she leaned back. Did Leila take the picture that she photographed of the star? Jill supposed the photo did belong to Leila. Leila was a photographer, and Jill knew they were funny about rights and stuff.

Leila had said she photographed the star. She had said the star was carved on a wooden floor in an old church. Jill recalled that Leila had gone over the details of the photo, something about evildoers. She re-

membered thinking again of former President Bush. One world order
and all. That's exactly what David had said when Allan was driving.
She thought again about her Remote Viewing of a group of men
that should never have been organized in such a fashion: Christians,
Muslims, Israelis, and Chechens. Jill flipped back in her notebook and
studied the word Ochrana and what else was mind-mapped on the
page: Russian oil, Operation Silhouette. Jill now knew that Operation
Silhouette was part of the Arab Spring.

She thought about what David had told her about the Gladios
of Istanbul and their brothers, the Chechen mafia. "Chechens," she
said out loud. Turning the page, she began to write notes and kicked
herself for not writing them down sooner. If she had written them
down when Leila first told her, then... Jill recalled the day they left Abu
Dhabi after Stan Brown was caught; their first stop was Brussels. They
went to find the old church. It was Leila who told Jill the church had
burned down and the wooden carving of the star was destroyed. Why
hadn't she questioned this before? Jill suddenly felt stupid.

Why would a church in Brussels burn down? Surely it wasn't made
of wood. Especially if it was old; as Leila had said, if a church were old,
it would not have been made of wood. Not in Brussels, anyway. Old
churches in most of Europe were made of stone. Jill felt like kicking
herself in the ass. She shoved her notebook across the desk, accidentally
pushing the pouch off the edge. It tumbled to the floor. Jill stood and
walked over to the minibar. It had been restocked, and she plucked
a bottle of water and cracked it open, pouring it into a plastic glass.
"Classy," she sniped as she sat back down and sipped.

She leaned forward and fingered the mouse again. If it was true,
Google must have something about a church burning down in Brussels. Jill had to find out. After several minutes of exhaustive searching,
she found nothing. Leila had said a man told her that the church had

burned down. Someone was lying, and it was beginning to look like that someone was Leila. But if Leila lied, then why?

Jill glanced at the clock on the nightstand: 22:05. Kali would still be at work now, she thought. She considered calling Eric to see if he had called about Leila, but she needed more information. Besides, he didn't seem to take her seriously when she first asked him to learn more about Leila. Jill would sound obsessed. She thought about that word and questioned herself again. "Obsessed describes me well," Jill said out loud. Then, with no further thought, she logged into the VPN. Let's start with Kali.

"A star?" Kali questioned.

"Yeah, remember that star I drew in my... ahem."

"You mean your non-Remote Viewing? Yeah, I remember. The Star of David, right? If I recall correctly, it wasn't the true Star of David, was it? Hang on." Jill could hear Kali's fingers tapping across a keyboard. "Ah, yes. Still have the notes. Why are you asking? Is everything okay? I mean, I know it's only been a few weeks since... since..." Kali trailed off.

Jill felt the guilt grumbling in her gut. But she needed time; she needed to find out what the hell was going on. She didn't have time to deal with guilt right now. Besides, she didn't have enough information and knew darn well Kali would question her like a drill sergeant. A barrage of questions would only muddy the waters right now. Kali would understand that much she knew. "I'm not sure why I'm asking, actually." This wasn't a lie. "I was just thinking about it. I was going over my notes when I saw my drawing of the star. The Star of David has six points, right? In your research, did you find any information about a four-pointed star?"

"Four points?" Kali sounded confused.

"Yes, like a point at the bottom, the top, and both sides equally. Kind of like a cross."

"A cross?" Kali asked, and Jill could picture one of Kali's eyebrows lifting.

Jill looked at what she had drawn. There was a circle around it. When Jill first looked at this, she thought it was part of her mind mapping. Plenty of lines and circles are present when using this technique. "Yeah, I guess it could be a star in the shape of a cross, sort of. I guess. And there may be a circle around it. I don't know for sure. Anyway, if you find something about this star symbol, can you drop me an email?"

"Are you RVing again? Where did you see this star, Jill?" Kali didn't pause for the answer; she kept going. "After all, you are in Turkey, and there's a star and a half moon on the Turkish flag. Well, more like a crescent moon than a circle."

Jill looked back at her drawing. "No, it's a full circle. Maybe it's nothing."

"Does this star have something to do with your money laundering case?"

Jill shrugged the question off. "I really don't know, just wondering, I guess. Any chance you can do some sleuthing about this drawing for me?"

"Ooh, okay, no probs, girl. So how are things going with your new assignment? Any good lookin'...?" Kali trailed off. "Sorry, I meant, how's it going?"

Jill thought about her question. She could answer truthfully this time because she hadn't known why she was sent to Turkey. But then she said, "It's going okay. I'm settling in." If you didn't count that David was alive somewhere in Turkey and that she watched a rogue Muslim woman kill a madam at a brothel several hours before while trying to rescue a twelve-year-old child from the sex trade. Hell, it was going great. Great.

"You got my email about Gabriella Smith? It's weird. I was at the Embassy getting processed for my visa and stuff, and I came across a girl."

"Girl? Listening." As if it were a hashtag. "You said this in your email, but it looked like you wrote it quickly. What's the scoop?"

Jill went through what happened, leaving out David and Yildiz. "I could use some help. No one seems to care about this girl. An American girl, only twelve."

Jill shuddered. "It's as if it's commonplace here. Young girls traded and performing sex for money are everywhere. I dunno."

"They probably will never see a dime." Kali's voice fumed. "How the hell did a twelve-year-old, let alone an American child, end up in a brothel in Turkey? FFS." Kali ended with an acronym, as she often did. "Anyway, I got your email first and sent it out on the wire looking for birth records. The parents' names will be a great help. Smith is a touchy one, as it is the most common last name in the US."

"There's something else. When she was at the Embassy, she kept repeating a number."

"Number?"

"There was a wretched woman who filled out the intake form. She told me about this number. Get a pen; it's a long one: 1376833626."

"Got it. Odd, though. Why would a twelve-year-old be reciting a long number like that?"

"I don't know. It could all just be gibberish, Kali. Can you check it out?"

"I'm on it! And I'll let you know what I find out about the star," Kali said before hanging up the phone.

CHAPTER FORTY-NINE

Jill shook her wet hair as she unveiled it from the towel. She looked at the computer, then at the bed, and sighed. Jill was tired now. She opened the minibar fridge, grabbed a bottle of water, and cracked it open. She sighed again, pouring the water into a plastic glass. Her robe felt warm as it began to take the chill off the day. She reached over for her mobile and thumbed it. No new messages. Taking her glass and mobile, she walked over to the bed and set them on the table. The warmth of the soft, tightly woven sheets hugged her.

Too much had happened today. Too much. Her call with Kali made Jill feel homesick. Maybe she was just tired of it all. David was gone again, and this small fact perturbed her this time. Clearly, what he did or didn't do was out of her control. She thought about the Gladios, the Bubbas, and the Chechens. Maybe he got his ass captured. But Jill didn't believe so. Those Tom and Jerrys would have known about it. Frankly, it seemed odd to Jill that they were not surprised she hadn't heard from him. Something else was amiss. Something else.

But right now, all Jill could think about was what happened in the brothel. Gabriella. And then there was Yildiz. Who was Yildiz? She was definitely more than just a Turkish PRO. Jill had profiled her in the van coming back from the brothel. Her physique was slight and willowy. But her moves were precise. She was trained. Krav Maga,

Israeli, Jill recalled. It was not an accident that she had killed that woman. She knew exactly what she was doing. Was killing that woman necessary? Surely she could have knocked the gun out of her hand. Surely. Maybe Jill was just pissed off about being unable to interrogate the woman. After all, she was clearly part of their vile operation. Jill wondered if she should call some authority. She recalled the two police officers in the souk alley. Her instinct told her they were not the sort of police she was used to, like in the US. She could have told Tweedle Dum and Tweedle Dee, but they were CIA, not local law enforcement. And the CIA shouldn't be operating as law enforcement in a foreign country. Sure, she knew that legally the Embassy, hell, even this residence, was considered to be on US soil. Her thought moved from Yildiz to Gabriella. Where had they taken her? Yildiz said she'd get in touch with Jill after she did some research. Research, what the hell did that mean? Jill didn't hold up much hope. Jill thumbed the phone and checked to see if Yildiz's number was saved. Yildiz. Jill sounded out the name Y I L D I Z. Putting her glass on the nightstand, she stood and moved toward her desk. She fingered the mouse, pulled up Google, typed "Yildiz = name," and hit enter. Jill sucked in a sharp breath through her nose as she read what was on the screen.

About the name Yildiz

The meaning of the name Yildiz: Star

The origin of the name Yildiz: Turkish

Jill looked down at her notebook where the lone four-point star was doodled earlier.

A star. Again, a star. Jill grabbed her pouch off the floor and marched over to the bed. With her notebook by her side, she propped up the pillows higher from her previous Remote View and sat. She spread her legs, opened the pouch, and dumped the clay tiles onto the bed.

She began to scribe.

Star

David

Star

Leila

Star

Yildiz

Star

Gabriella

Star

Gabriella

Star

Gabriella

After she wrote her starting number ending with the digit one, she instinctively moved the clay tiles around with her left hand. "Where are you, Gabriella? Where are you?" Jill whispered. She continued her chant, moving slowly into a meditative state.

"Star. David. Star. Leila. Star. Yildiz. Star. Gabriella. Star. Gabriella. Star. Gabriella. Where are you, Gabriella? Where are you?" Over and over and over.

The cement building was cold and damp. A light blinked on and off in a small enclosed room in the far corner. With it came a sound. "Beep. Whoosh. Beep. Whoosh. Beep ..." The sound continued. Suddenly, a light came on, and a dark shadow—a tall, thin shadow—moved around the clouded, glassed room. "Beep. Whoosh. Beep. Whoosh. Beep ..." In the distance, sounds indicated that heavy equipment was being moved around. As she moved closer toward the lit room, the silhouette turned. It had breasts. The shadow was that of a woman. "Beep. Whoosh. Beep. Whoosh. Beep ..." The sound changed. It was now a moan. It came from the room where the figure was moving around. There it was again. A moan, a moan from a child. Like a child having a nightmare when they can't wake up. The moan was interrupted. "Beep. Whoosh. Beep. Whoosh. Beep ..." The sound was speeding up now. "Beep. Whoosh. Beep. Whoosh. Beep ...." Another light flicked on in a different room beside the first one. The smell of cigar smoke lingered. Inside she heard voices—voices of men.

Suddenly, bright lights flickered and hummed, illuminating the whole building. A giant symbol was on the wall beside the door where the men spoke. A star. A four-pointed star. The searing pain kicked in. Where was the pain coming from? Pain. Have to go. Have to go. Have to go now. A blinding light flashed, and a dark image began to fade in. Menacing eyes pierced through first. Pain. Hatred. Those eyes. Those eyes. David's eyes.

CHAPTER FIFTY

Jill frantically grabbed at the air. "Eh, eh, eh," she huffed, trying to understand where she was. Jill sat up. The bedside lamp glowed, lighting up the bed. It was always disorienting for Jill when coming out of an RV session, but this RV was strong. Jill grabbed her notebook, looked at the ideogram she had drawn, picked up the pen, and began writing. Her hand was shaking so badly that she didn't know if she could read her writing.

warehouse

cement

cold

dark

light

sounds

a machine, like an ICU machine in a hospital

equipment moving

men talking

a child moaning or two children

David

pain

She laid the pen down. Usually, the Remote Viewer was not part of the scene in the RV. But instead, it was like watching a movie playing before her. David. Why the hell was David in her RV? His eyes were full of hate. Full of hatred for whom? Jill wondered. She knew she had to be careful with Remote Viewing, especially alone. Eric had warned her that the viewer's thoughts and feelings could sometimes skew a session. She had to be careful not to fill in the blanks.

But what she did know—what she had always known—was to trust her RVs and, more importantly, her intuition. It's why Jill had been the top viewer at the FBI. Before Matthew McGregor, anyway.

Jill sat in silence and looked over what she had written. Were these results about Gabriella? David? She hadn't seen Gabriella in the RV. But David was there. She was sure about that. His hatred was seething. She felt it—felt it in the pit of her stomach.

Jill looked over at the alarm clock. It was 23:47. Was David back yet? She thought about what David had told her when she saw him at the airport in Tucson. He said someone was following them. Then a thought struck her hard, as if getting hit over the head with a blunt object, shaking loose parts of her brain. Jill jolted up as she felt something move. She held her breath and watched as the room began to turn. She knew it was coming; she'd felt it before. The PTSD pushed the plunger into the spinning room. She had to get breathing. She had to stop it before it went into a full-blown panic attack. But it was spinning too fast now. The world was spinning out of control—Jill's world.

CHAPTER FIFTY-ONE

Matthew looked across the desk, zombie-like, as the doctor spoke. "I see you've refused to take your meds; it's why we've been injecting you with your medicine. It appears to be having a positive effect on you. Don't you feel it?" The doctor flipped through a file. "How are you feeling now?"

Matthew was shackled, his wrists to his ankles. He looked through the doctor and wondered when this quack would let him go back to his refuge—his prison cell. He shrugged and nodded. "Yeah. Stop with the needles now."

The doctor studied him. "I'm not so sure that's a good idea, Matthew. Let's have a chat, shall we? According to this file,"—the doctor held up the manila folder with a bright-red stamp that read "Sealed."—"Yes, I could access your juvenile file. According to it, you managed to kill your mother at the age of twelve."

Matthew didn't move. "Of course, you can't be blamed for the dissociative disorder. It was why you spent most of your life in a mental facility. They thought they had rehabilitated you, of course, and discharged you at age twenty-one. Well, that was until you began constructing that killing cave."

Matthew stared at him blankly, unamused.

"It's important to know, Matthew, that not taking your meds will continue to aid you in a downward spiral. We are aware from our studies that patients with your disorder think that when they feel healthy, they are cured. There is no cure, Matthew. You will have to take them for the rest of your life."

All Matthew heard was, "Blah, blah, blah." His mind was elsewhere. He was concentrating on something else. He felt as if he was not in his body. The energy running through him was so intense; he felt electrified. He could see things. He could always see things. When he was younger, it was cool. Now what he felt and saw in his visions seemed clear to him. He needed to find Jill Oliver; they said she was his final victim. Final? Who said she was his final victim? These quacks couldn't keep him here forever. Besides, he had fun in his dreams.

"Blah, blah, blah," he heard the doctor say. These days his dreams were filled with Jill Oliver, but the last one was very vivid. And somehow, he wanted to tell her. Tell her to be careful. Tt. Tt. Tt. The letters floated around and around in his head and sometimes bumped into each other. He wanted her to be careful. He needed her to be careful. After all, he wanted her to stay alive. Stay alive so he could see her again one day. This thought excited him. But the goddamn medicine they were needling him with kept his erection at bay.

"Tell me why Jill Oliver is so important to you now?" This pulled Matthew's attention. "You have to be careful not to become obsessive with your thoughts of her. It's a sign of regression, not understanding or comprehending your reality."

Matthew sat up. "My reality? What do you mean, my reality?" His wrist shackles rattled as he tried to separate his arms.

"Tell me then, Matthew, what is your perceived reality?"

Matthew thought about it. In his last dream, he saw Jill. Saw her being shot, but he couldn't see the shooter. But one thing was sure.

She knew the killer. But how could he tell the doctor this? How could he disclose his fantasies to the doctor? About slicing each of Jill's nipples slowly and methodically with his surgical knife, watching her and listening to her screams as he pleasured himself.

CHAPTER FIFTY-TWO

Jill breathed as she retched again in the wastebasket beside her bed. She had the dry heaves now. The room had stopped spinning after her last full vomit. She had these attacks less frequently after marrying David. It was hard to remember the last time she had a full-blown attack. With David, she felt safe. But now, who the hell knew? Jill slowly stood, got her bearings, and walked over to her desk. The sound of an email arriving pinged.

Jill,

Please call me as soon as you get this message. It's important.

Eric

The time on the email was just several minutes ago. It was late in Virginia. Jill pulled up her VoIP phone and dialed. "Wallace," he answered on the first ring.

"Hi Eric, it's Jill. I just got your message, and it sounded like you needed to speak to me urgently. I was going to call you anyway."

Eric interjected, "Remember you asked me about Leila Sorel?" Jill stiffened. "Well, the Bureau has been asking our team to see if we could RV on people as targets instead of just structures. As you know, I've always been hesitant about this. I'd hate to give the wrong intel on a person and classify them as something they are not. Not in today's day and age, anyway."

"Yeah, I know. But what does that have to do with Leila?"

"Well, I needed to do some testing on viewing people instead of structures. You know, checking false positives and all on non-threats. So the team did an RV today."

"Yeah, and...?"

"They RV'd Leila." Jill's nose whistled as she sucked in a breath. "Normally, a Remote View would determine location. Nothing more."

"What happened? Who did the RV?"

"The team: Mitch, Malcolm, Jen, and this new kid Bert. He's quite good."

"What were the results?" Jill asked anxiously.

"They didn't know that you know Miss Sorel."

Jill thought about what the agents had asked her. How well do you know Leila Sorel? Eric interrupted her thought. "Do you have a pen, Jill? I can give you preliminary results. And since it was a test sort of thing off the record, it's not classified."

"Standby." Jill went to the bed, grabbed her notebook and pen, then returned to the desk and opened the notebook to where she had just written her RV notes. On the left side of the notebook, she wrote the words "Leila RV" and underlined them.

hangar

cement

cold

dark

airplanes

alarm clock

Jill looked at the notes Eric had just dictated to her; then she looked back at her notes she had written just a few minutes earlier from her RV session and coughed out a nervous choke.

Eric continued. "And there's one other thing. I struggled with whether to tell you about it. Mitch went into bi-location. You know, being in two places at the same time. Well... well, he wrote down the name of another person. A man. No one else in the group wrote a person's name."

"Who is it?" Jill demanded.

"Matthew McGregor."

The whir of an engine started to scream in Jill's ears, an engine that began the tilt-a-whirl back up. Jill ripped off her headset and tried desperately to stop the world from spinning again. Strands of hair punched through Jill's fingers as she pulled on her hair, wanting to steady herself.

"Jill? Jill?" The sounds of a mouse calling her name through the phone. Why was she losing it for the second time in one hour? What was happening to her? She recalled what the doctor had told her to do when she was feeling a panic attack coming. She thought about all those years of nightmares—of screaming dreams. Dreams about hell. Screams in dreams about being held captive by him. Matthew McGregor.

"Screw you, Matthew McGregor," she barked. "Screw you, Matthew McGregor," she exhaled in a breathy bravado as she picked up the headset and placed it over her head.

"Jill?"

"Are you serious, Eric? Mitch wrote his name?"

"Yes."

"Why would he come up in an RV about Leila?" Jill studied the notes that Eric had just given her again. She couldn't bring herself to write down his name. Jill rolled her thoughts around. "Maybe for some crazy reason, Leila is interviewing him for some story or something." Jill felt a blade of pain in her back.

"That was my first thought, so I inquired. You know, the kind. Anyway, he's not in the general population. He's in isolation. He's only allowed one visitor every two weeks, and according to the logs, that author Maxter is the only one that has been in to visit him."

"What else did Mitch say about him? I mean, with his name. What were the visions around his name?"

"I asked Mitch, and he kept saying that Matthew McGregor was at an airport." Eric sighed. "I really don't know, Jill. It's truly an anomaly, I guess. As I said, it was a test, and there is no way he could be at an airport, not to mention with Leila Sorel. I wouldn't read too much into it. I'm not sure if any of this helps with your question about Leila, but it was interesting, that's for sure. Another reason why we should not implement Remote Viewing of people. Anyway, it's in my report."

Jill's mind was seeping into the tunnels, and she wasn't listening to Eric's ramblings about his report. "Okay, Eric," she said half-heartedly. "Thanks for the information ... I think."

"It's all I got for you. I called some folks in the know, and there was nothing surreptitious about Leila that they could find."

"It's okay, Eric. I ... I gotta go." The sound of her mobile phone vibrating on the nightstand ended her call.

CHAPTER
FIFTY-THREE

Jill snatched up the phone and swiped hello. An abrupt voice bellowed, "Jill, it's Yildiz." She sounded off-key. "I've got some information for you. I'm on my way to your, ah... residence." The sounds of honking horns beeped in the background.

"Gabriella, you've found Gabriella?"

"Well, not exactly. But yes, I may know where she is now."

"Where?" Jill interrupted.

"I have asked many people and have just got word," said Yildiz. "We must hurry, and it will be very dangerous there. You know, there is a lot of security right now because of IS."

"IS?"

"Yes, the Islamic State."

Jill knew the Islamic state; hell, everyone with a television knew. "I see. I hadn't heard of this term before. ISIS, ISIL, yes."

"I will be there in ten minutes."

"Where are we going, Yildiz?" Jill demanded.

"A hangar. A hangar at Antalya airport. It's a smaller airport that mainly military use."

Jill squeezed out a breath, almost stumbling over her feet as she rushed to pick up her notebook, eyeing the words "airplanes" and "hangar" from Mitch.

"Okay, Yildiz, but I will need a weapon. A gun," Jill barked before she hung up.

Jill sat and swiped the mouse of the computer. Yildiz. Star. "There is no way I can trust you, Yildiz." Jill thought about it some more. She thought about calling Eric back and telling him everything. But what could he do? Besides, they were just going to an airport hangar; she would have a weapon if Yildiz came through. She hoped David would return from his "theory" trip. But Yildiz, yes. She'd have to be careful. Besides, what was she really looking for at David's bidding? The message to David from Yildiz that Jill had stolen a peek at said she'd found what David was looking for. What could that be?

Jill opened the email from Kali, hit reply, and wrote a blurb about Yildiz.

Kali,

Have a lead on Gabriella. I met an intelligence broker at the Embassy. Name is Yildiz Aslan. We are going to a hangar at Antalya airport. See what you can find out about her and reference the star icon. I know, I know. Just please do it.

J

Jill walked to the bathroom, splashed some water on her face, and chugged a gulp of water. "Okay, Yildiz, let's see who you really are."

CHAPTER FIFTY-FOUR

"Here," Yildiz said as she passed a Sig to Jill. "I did some checking on you after our event at the brothel. I know you know how to use it," she said vaguely.

Jill released the magazine, counted the bullets, popped it back in, and racked the slide. "What are we facing? What did your intel say about why we should go there?"

Yildiz looked at the driver and then back to Jill. "We must be very careful," she whispered. "I know these people. They are not good people."

"Who are they? How do you know Gabriella is there?"

"Gabriella? I am not sure if she is there." The car took a sharp right, and Jill leaned into Yildiz.

"Then why the hell are we going?" A niggle of suspicion circled Jill's periphery. She held the gun firmly as it rested on her lap.

"We are going to Terminal Five. It is separate from the main terminal. This terminal is for cargo." Jill listened intently. "My source is vetted. He said there was a shipment leaving tonight."

"A shipment?"

"The girl in the brothel said the girls were being shipped somewhere."

Jill's brow furrowed, trying to follow Yildiz. "He said the shipment was one of their regular drug shipments. They use it to fund their projects. This shipment also has live packages."

"Packages?"

"Children," Yildiz said matter-of-factly. "The shipment includes children."

Jill pinched the bridge of her nose between her brows. "How can they transport drugs and children so easily? Where is the shipment going?"

Yildiz didn't miss a beat. "The shipment, I have been told, is going to the United States. America."

CHAPTER FIFTY-FIVE

"This may be the last time we meet like this." The fat man took a pull on his cigar, addressing six men who sat around the table.

"What we are about to do will be discussed for many years. They will not have seen this coming. Once we have the shipment's funds, we will proceed with the operation." The men nodded in unison.

The quiet man who hadn't said much cleared his throat to speak. He typically didn't say much, but this was his contribution to the group. "The device is in place now. It is fully enriched. We will pay the smugglers as agreed. The areas we have targeted in Europe are beginning to unravel as we speak. The key officials who help loosen the borders have complied. Once we ignite the device, there will be an upheaval that the world has never seen before."

The fat man stood and looked at each member of the room. "What our brother here has said is true. Blowing up the Mosul dam will kill over one and a half million Iraqis." The men looked around at each other as if hearing this for the first time. "Our earlier speculation was not accurate. Over twelve billion cubic meters of water will be released. The dam will cause floodwaters up to fifteen meters high. Our NATO brothers have boots on the ground and are silently urging officials to give warnings to their citizens. But this problem, my brothers, is out of our hands. We must flood the oil fields along the Tigris River and as far south as Baghdad, and because it will affect Syria, our sleepers in Europe will be woken with a super-sized alarm clock."

The Arab man stood. "We must go forward, insha'Allah. When we control the Russian oil, we will control the world."

The two Chechen brothers stood. "Hamdoola! Praise be to God." Chairs scraped as the other men stood, and as if in a masterful theater performance, they chanted, "Ochrana."

CHAPTER FIFTY-SIX

The night had no moonlight as they pulled up to a large field on the side of a dirt road. A large fence lined the field with barbed wire rolled in a tight tube and sitting atop it.

"Where are we?" Jill asked.

Yildiz nodded at the driver, exited the van, and Jill followed. "We have to go this way. It is our only chance to get in without being seen."

Jill looked down the high fence line.

"How are we supposed to get in?"

Yildiz pulled a wire cutter from the side pocket of her black fatigues. "I had been thinking about this since I learned of this location. We will cut through the chain links; they are flimsy enough. We must first find a dark area to cut." They looked down the fence line and spotted a pole with no light illuminating it. They walked just far enough from the other lights not to be seen and stopped when they found a dark spot in the fence. Yildiz bit into the wire, methodically clipping as Jill pulled back the newly formed flap.

"This should be big enough," Yildiz said as she crouched through the two-foot opening. Jill followed. Standing inside the fenced field, Jill studied Yildiz as she moved. She was doing her surveillance, similar to how Jill did hers.

Jill did her scans, but there wasn't much to see in the empty field.

"Come," Yildiz commanded softly. They skulked across the field and onto a paved tarmac. Jill scanned the buildings. There was only one hangar that appeared to have any activity. When they reached the cement hangar, Jill heard machinery moving around.

They flashed their backs flat against the concrete building as they crab-walked to the edge and peered around the corner. Two men stood talking; one was smoking. They looked in the opposite direction as if surveying something in the distance. The man on the right had his back to them. But there was something familiar about him. Maybe it was how he leaned on his right leg, showing his dominance, just off to one side. One of the men turned and walked toward a black SUV, jumped into it, and U-turned away. Yildiz nudged Jill as the other man turned. His blond, shoulder-length hair blew back in the slight breeze. The man was David. David turned and looked in their direction as if sensing their presence. There was no way he could see them; it was too dark. Then he turned and walked through the open hangar door. Jill caught her breath and whispered, "What the hell?" They backed up, squaring their shoulders against the cold wall. Jill held her gun, elbows bent, resting it against her left shoulder.

"Fuck," cursed Jill. Yildiz nodded. "What was the intel, Yildiz? Who told you about this place? What did they say to you? Did they say who was making the shipment? That's David, for goddamn sake." Yildiz didn't respond. It was evident to Jill she was considering something. "What!" Jill barked.

"So this is why," Yildiz breathed, looking deep in thought.

"Why what?" Jill was beginning to come unraveled. "Why what, Yildiz? Is this the right place where the shipment was leaving? I mean...are you sure?"

"Yes."

Thoughts swirled too fast in Jill's head. But... how could David be involved in human trafficking? He couldn't be. And without any further thought, images flashed in Jill's mind like a giant IMAX theater—David at the Embassy with a nonchalant response about the child. David not believing there even was a child. The way that bitch smirked at Jill when David was asking questions about Gabriella. David didn't care. David didn't care about a child. About Jill. Bastard.

"Jill. Jill." Jill swiped Yildiz's hand off her shoulder.

"Don't touch me," Jill barked a little too loudly.

"Stop it," Yildiz hushed, standing squarely before Jill. "You need to contain your emotions. These are dangerous people—Gladios and maybe even the Bubbas. Be quiet. Be quiet now, or we will leave."

Jill squeezed the butt of the gun tighter and took a deep breath. "The Gladios...."

"Sssh. Let us go."

They continued crab-walking around the corner, their backs against the wall, and inched their way to the door. A small light above the open doorway made them vulnerable to whoever was inside. Slowly, Yildiz moved her covered head and periscoped the entrance. She slowly walked into the hangar. Jill followed and stumbled when she saw the room. They stood just inside the large cement building. It was the same building as Jill's last RV. The same beeping sounds echoed in the empty hangar. Jill's eyes landed on a lit room surrounded by dark glass. She moved slowly toward it, her back close to the wall. Yildiz followed her. As they approached, a symbol on the wall beside the door became clear. It was a picture of a star.

Yildiz hushed, "The Gladios."

"What?" Jill said, surprised. "You know what this symbol is?" She stared at the four-pointed star. "The Gladios?"

"Yes," Yildiz whispered. "I knew it would be them with this type of shipment. But why is this..." Yildiz brushed her fingers over the painted symbol. "Why would they paint this here?" Yildiz turned around, surveying their surroundings. To the right of the symbol was a door.

Yildiz began to move in the door's direction when Jill whispered, "Wait."

Yildiz looked back at Jill, who was tilting her head toward the bright, frosted-glass room door.

Yildiz pressed her ear against the door, following Jill's lead. The beeping sound was consistent. "Beep. Whoosh. Beep. Whoosh." Jill nodded, gesturing toward the doorknob. She slowly twisted the knob and pushed the door open. Jill stepped into the room and froze. Yildiz pushed past her and abruptly stopped.

The room that was masked as a small office was vast. Airplane shipping containers were stacked at least twelve feet high and had the word FEMA stamped on them. But what was in the rest of the large room stunted their movement.

The floor was lined with wooden pallets. On top of the pallets were coffin-like boxes. One by one by one by one, all in a row. At the end of the row was a large pump with tubes snaking from it. The machine beeped consistently, pumping something into each little box. Jill slowly approached, still trying to assess what she was seeing. Then she heard it—a moan. Yildiz moved toward Jill. She must have heard it too. Jill leaned down and looked into the end of one box. The end had two small grates that looked like they came from small prison windows. She wished she had a flashlight to look in. She tried to focus her brain on what she was seeing. It... it... it was hair—blonde hair.

"Eh, eh, eh." The hair shivered slightly as a slight moan echoed inside. A child. It was a goddamn child, imprisoned in a coffin, alive. Jill stood and began counting the boxes when Yildiz spun around and froze. Jill twisted around at the sound of Yildiz's movement and calculated her Weaver stance. Jill pointed her gun at shoulder height, past Yildiz, at David.

CHAPTER
FIFTY-SEVEN

More moans began to echo as the three stood calculating each other. David stood with his feet shoulder-width apart and held a pistol at his waist, pointing it at them. Jill's hand wobbled as she grasped the intensity of the situation. Would Jill be able to shoot him—kill David, kill her husband? She did not know.

"You couldn't leave it alone, Jill. You just had to find that girl."

This stung Jill, drop-kicking her in the heart. "What is going on, David? Why are you here?" That was a dumb question; she impulsively blurted it out. But she didn't know what else to say—what else to do. Adrenaline kept her hands from shaking as the cognizance of who David really was came tumbling in. Jill squared her shoulders tight. "Put the gun down, David. Put it down, or I swear I'll shoot."

David just smirked at her. His right eyebrow lifted as his lips curled. The door behind him began to open, and from the shadow, a figure emerged. Holding a Sig, the same as Jill. A female voice said, "No, Jill, you drop your gun, or I'll shoot your freakin' head off." Leila moved out of the shadow and stood next to David.

Jill blinked. "Leila!"

"Don't look so shocked, Jill. Come on, even you can't be that dumb," her Asian green eyes narrowed.

Jill moved her aim from David to Leila, then back to David. Yildiz stood still, and at that moment, a niggle began to scratch. Then it started tapping Jill on the shoulder. Was she fighting against two people or three? She had to think. Survive. She profiled the situation as if running a race. Yildiz—no gun, but she would have a knife. Two o'clock, David's gun. Three o'clock, Leila's gun. Three on one? Maybe she'd get one of them. Jill didn't know if Leila knew how to shoot, but she sure as hell looked like she did. And if Yildiz was one of them, then she had no chance. No chance in hell. Jill said what instinctively came to her mind. She needed time. She needed a distraction. "Children. You're selling children!"

"Psst, they're just a commodity," meowed Leila. "It's a means to an end, is all. It's what we do." She tilted her head towards David. "It's not what gives us the big bucks, though." Leila lifted her chin in the direction of the FEMA-labeled containers.

Jill knew it was heroin and continued. "But they're just children... kids, Leila. Do you know what they will do to them? You claim you work for the CIA, but now you sell children?"

"Who do you think pays us, you moron?" Jill's hand wobbled. "Who do you think pays for the Gladios? How do you believe we can operate, doing what needs to be done?"

Jill's brow furrowed. "So you are a Gladio now? Really, Leila, how do you expect me to believe that?"

"I don't care what you think. I'll tell you one thing: you almost figured it out in Germany when you drew that star. Lucky for us, it wasn't a replica of our star—the Gladio star. And even luckier is how gullible you are. All I had to do was show you the Star of David, and you believed it. All of it. Couldn't have you working your juju shit, figuring out who Ochrana really is."

Jill stood stunned, then David spoke. "Go ahead, Lei, it doesn't matter; you can tell her. She won't be around to tell anyone." Jill saw Yildiz tense. "Let's watch them figure it out—figure it all out. Call it rude awakening 101." David smirked.

"With pleasure. I've been waiting for Miss Pollyanna to hear the truth. Can you imagine how hard it was for me not to tell you, Jill, that you had no idea what you were doing, supposedly looking for David in Dubai? L-O-L." David chuckled as he spelled out the acronym for "laugh out loud" for effect. "And when I'm done, I will shoot your Indian ass right in the head. You see, Jill, things in the world are not always what the media makes them out to be. In fact, most media outlets are working with us. Do you think what is happening in Syria, you know, with ISIS, is real? Give your head a shake. We're the ones who are pulling the strings. Remember your Remote Viewing of the men at the table? Ochrana. You got that one right. But poor Jill, weeping endlessly over David in that last RV in Dubai. Poor thing. You got that one wrong. David's dead, wah wah wah." Leila sneered out a laugh. "It was hard not to laugh at your pathetic self."

Yildiz took a step in Leila's direction. Leila kept the gun trained on Jill. "I wouldn't move any closer, you spook," Leila spat toward Yildiz. But Yildiz took another step towards her anyway, then stopped. Jill watched as Yildiz calculated.

Leila kept talking. "Now we're all here together. Maybe we should have a pity party. Isn't that why you're here anyway?" Jill didn't speak. She was busy staring at Leila's trigger finger. She was watching for any movement. "It's what we do. Our mission—well, this one is anyway. We destabilize the area, and we are doing that well here. This money—the money from this shipment—will fund our next operation.

Taking out the president of Turkey is only the beginning. But you won't be alive to witness the takedown of this nation. You won't be alive when we take down the Middle East."

Jill saw it. It was a slight tensing of Yildiz's right butt cheek. It was fast. Too fast for David. Too fast for Jill. Too fast, as Yildiz swung her leg at mach speed as she twisted. Her boot hit Leila's hand so hard that the gun flew against the machine pumping gas into the coffins and deactivated it. It clattered to the floor. Leila screamed as Yildiz's right leg was grounded on the floor. Yildiz jumped and twisted, pirouetting 360 degrees, and her left swung fast and nailed the gun out of David's hand. The gun skittered across the cement floor. But before she could plant her feet securely, Leila jumped onto Yildiz's back, screaming, "Bitch!" as she pulled the hijab off of Yildiz's head and began punching Yildiz repeatedly. One fist punch after the other hit the side of Yildiz's face. Yildiz's hair was long and whipped as she swung her left arm around, elbowed Leila in the chin, and then pinned Leila's punching arm. The move brought Leila's head forward. And in the same movement, like the rat-a-tat-tat of a machine gun, Yildiz brought her right fist up and gave Leila an uppercut to the chin, knocking Leila off balance before Yildiz jammed her right knee into Leila's sternum several times. Leila crumpled onto the cold floor, grasping at her chest. The move was so fast Jill could not react.

David lunged towards Yildiz. Jill shouted, "Stop, or I will shoot." But it was too late. With the butt of her hand, Yildiz sliced through David's advance. His head flew back as Yildiz's strike connected with David's nose. Yildiz grabbed and held his head, then lifted her right knee, connecting it with David's groin. He went down on his knees, and he pawed at his groin. Jill watched David yell something inaudible as Yildiz jumped high and gave him a roundhouse kick that snapped his head sideways. His head smacked hard as it hit the floor.

Barely breathing heavily, Yildiz pulled out a knife she had sheathed under her clothing and wiped her lips with the back of her hand. She moved towards Leila, who was belly-inching towards the door. Yildiz picked up her hijab, which was crumpled on the floor, and wrapped it around her neck. She straddled Leila, grabbed her hair, and yanked her head backward while she placed her left foot on Leila's back, pinning her.

"Stop," Jill shouted and aimed.

"Stay out of my business, Jill. This is my country she is attempting to destroy. My religion, she shows no respect for. But don't worry, Jill. I won't hurt her."

Jill breathed out, and for a split second, she thought of... but that split second caught Jill by surprise. She watched as Yildiz hacked a swift line through Leila's jugular. Blood sprayed, painting the door. Leila's head hitting the concrete floor was loud but not loud enough to drown out the sound of a gun's hammer being cocked. The metal was cold as it touched Jill's ear. A fat hand reached forward and grabbed the gun from Jill's hand.

CHAPTER FIFTY-EIGHT

David moaned as he came around from being knocked out. "Move," Stan Brown barked, pushing Jill's shoulder. Jill stumbled forward toward Yildiz. "Turn around and look at me. Both of you," his gravelly voice commanded.

Jill turned. Yup, of course, it was Stan Brown. This day couldn't get any worse. Stan was alive. The fat bastard stood, his tomato-like body plopping as he spoke. "Well. Well. Jill, we meet again," he hacked out the words. Jill watched as Stan looked down at Leila's limp body. Her hair was now matted with sticky blood. "I should thank you. Miss... Miss..." Stan pointed the gun at Yildiz's head.

"Aslan," she answered.

"Well, Miss Aslan, thank you. She had to go anyway. She was, how do you say ... getting too big for her britches," he drawled. David began to sit up, and he looked bewildered. "Get up," Stan barked. "Get up and grab that gun." He nodded toward where the gun lay. David blinked, grabbed his chin, slowly stood, walked over, and picked it up. He turned and held the gun at his waist, pointing it toward the two women.

"What are we to do now?" Stan smirked at them. "The two of you interrupting this shipment." He looked over at David. "How could you let this happen? You said she was contained, just here to keep the CIA's eyes off you."

"I ... uh ... I have no idea how she found this place. How could she know?" He paused and looked at Yildiz. "It was her. Yildiz." David gestured with his gun hand in Yildiz's direction. "She must have told her. There are spies everywhere in this shithole country."

Jill watched Yildiz tense. Jill looked at Stan's fat finger on the trigger and blurted, "How the hell did you get out of Guantanamo?" Jill knew it was a weak attempt to distract from what was inevitably going to happen.

"Oh, Jill, you have much to learn about your employer. Too bad you won't have time to learn such valuable lessons. I will give you the CliffsNotes version."

"What, from the US Marshals?" But she knew what he meant.

Stan frowned. "VIPs in the US government, you stupid girl." Stan gave an eye roll in David's direction. "For the record, I was treated very well at Gitmo. The royal treatment, actually."

"They said you were dead."

"Yes, that was a good story."

Jill caught David nodding his head, and if she were any closer to him, she'd grab it with both her hands and knee it to the moon. Suddenly, it happened. Jill had tried to control herself, but it was all too much now. Jill spewed at David, "You were always working with him. How could you, David? How could you work against your government? How could you sell children? For money? For goddamn money!" Jill spat, her voice going off-key.

David looked amused. Stan spoke first. "There are some things that are thicker than blood, Jill. He's not stupid. He knows the plan—understands the future of a world that needs a leader. It's not just about the money, although money gives us great options. David is part of the future. He is part of our group. The future is bigger than just a simple-minded deplorable like you. David knows what needs to be done. After all, he is my son. I've raised him to understand what is important."

While Stan spoke, Jill assessed the scene. David and Stan stood three feet apart, at least eight feet from where she and Yildiz stood. It was at that moment she realized Yildiz still held her knife. Blood dripped off the steel blade and pooled beside her right boot. But there was a problem; Yildiz was too far away to make any sort of Krav Maga, a ninja-type move. Jill wondered if Yildiz could throw a knife accurately. Jill had to be ready in case she did. It would happen fast; that much she knew.

Jill calculated the scenario. And as if Stan read her mind, he said, "Drop it, Miss Aslan. Drop the knife now." The steel blade clanged when it hit the cement floor.

Jill blurted, "You know you will be stopped! There is no way you can overtake the US government. Your plan is stupid!"

"Ah, Jill," he drawled as his lips curled. "There you go again, making moronic statements. You think it's a coincidence that all the Syrian refugees' primary destination is Germany? That is us, too. It's all planned. Our group, Ochrana, has been planning since before World War Two. We will complete its goals with the help of the Gladio Operation. We will take Turkey first, then Syria, and we will seize the Russian oil. Russia is a perfect scapegoat."

"Scapegoat?" Yildiz whispered.

Stan ignored her and continued. "It's too easy, really. The US will blame Russia or make it look like they do." He smirked at David. "You can't stop it now. You can't stop us now."

Jill noticed David's weight shift from the left to his right. Was he getting ready to shoot her? Stan continued. "We have a plan in place.

We will take over the world banks while the US and Russia fight. Many people will die, but in the end, we will have the power. We will have a new world order." And with that statement, Stan and David chanted, "Ochrana!"

The sounds of children moaning interrupted the exchange. They were coming out of their drug-induced state. This caught Stan's attention. "We must end this, David. We must end this now. You know what to do."

Jill and Yildiz tensed in unison. Jill saw Yildiz glance down at the knife. She was going to grab it. "I sure do," David barked, catching Jill's attention. Jill didn't understand. Jill didn't comprehend. It happened so fast; she didn't have time to move. David lifted the gun and pointed it at her before twisting on his right foot and shooting Stan Brown in the side of his head.

EPILOGUE

The plane bumped over cumulus clouds as it crossed the jet stream on its way to Washington, DC.

"Only one hour more," Jill Oliver said as she looked down at the dark-haired girl who sat beside her in the oversized seat.

"I'm afraid," Gabby whispered. "What happens if he doesn't like me?"

Jill reached over and put her hand on Gabriella's. "It will be okay. Everything will be okay now." Okay, Jill thought to herself. Would anything ever be okay again? Too much had happened. Too much. Jill watched Gabriella squirm slightly as she pulled her hand off Gabriella's. One thing Jill knew for sure—maybe the only thing she knew for sure—was that Gabriella Smith would be okay.

Kali had come through using the ten-digit number and Sophia and James Smith in her search. She got a hit. Not a hit in the National Birth Records database, however, but a hit in the one used at the NSA. The ten-digit number was a security clearance number. Every agent had one, and the more numbers, the higher the security clearance.

Gabriella Smith was actually Gabriella Read, the daughter of Trace Read. The irony of Mr. and Mrs. Smith was lost on Jill when Kali chimed in with it. Kali had learned that Gabriella's father was alive. She knew that about eight years ago, while deep undercover, Trace was shot. The report stated he was left for dead, and when the team came to extract his body, Trace was alive. "Barely," Kali put in. He remained in a coma for several years before regaining consciousness. By then, Sophia had already moved back to Italy with Gabriella. Kali had asked Eric to call Trace directly when she couldn't reach Jill, who was busy trying not to get her ass shot by David. "I should have kicked your ass for not telling me," Kali spouted.

After several discussions between Trace and Eric and receiving his documents verifying that Trace was indeed Gabriella's father, Eric was sure that he was. He explained the situation to Trace. It turned out that Trace had gone to Italy in an attempt to find his wife and daughter. But with the last name of Smith, it was futile. "Apparently, he wrote the Italian Embassy monthly with his concern about finding his wife and child," Kali added. "But no one would help him."

He was thankful that Jill was escorting Gabriella back to her home country. Kali had also arranged for a child psychologist to be present with Trace upon their arrival.

Jill looked at the large screen before her and watched as the mapped plane looped around Baltimore and began its descent. As her ears started to pop, releasing pressure, she thought of David. Moments after David had shot and killed Stan, a siege of Turkish police swarmed the hangar. All three were detained and taken into custody. It took over nine hours of interrogation before they had the necessary documentation to release Jill. The children were recovered and sent to a local hospital under the guardianship of CACU. All had survived.

Ian and Todd had sent a special convoy to escort Jill back to the Embassy. They had confirmed to Jill that both David and Leila were under CIA investigation. But it was David who gave the CIA investigator all of what he knew. The Ochrana group was immediately apprehended. "The interrogation is ongoing," Todd had piped up. David had also given the specific details of their plan to blow up the dam in Mosul, Iraq. "We're hoping that others in the group will spill what they know. Who and where all the actors are," Todd concluded.

When Jill asked about David and what would happen to him now as a traitor, both agents looked dumbfounded. "You don't know?" asked Ian.

"Know what?"

Ian had already made several calls and successfully increased Jill's security clearance. "David... well, David is a black operative. Deep undercover for the US government." They told Jill that they hadn't known this information until the big bust at the hangar. "His target was Stan Brown and the Ochrana group," Ian stated, continuing to tell Jill about David's mission. David knew that Stan was not at Gitmo and was still alive. "He was also right about Allan, but Allan wasn't working with Stan's group. Instead, he was a double agent for the Gladios. He had to do some things that would be considered harsh, but he has been completely exonerated. His superiors were commending David for successfully infiltrating the Ochrana group meetings. It was too soon for a sting, according to David, but the children made him pull the trigger on the operation ahead of time. He drew the line at risking the health and lives of children.

At that point, tears began to plop on Jill's cheeks. She hadn't planned to cry. She finally had her answer. It was all too much. And when she asked about Leila, the two agents shifted from pride to menace. Todd explained that Leila had committed acts of treason. He said the CIA had plenty of evidence to convict her. It was just a matter of time. "She got greedy," Ian added. "Greedy and careless, selling children. She had sold out to the wrong person."

"Who?" Jill queried.

"David," Todd answered. "If she hadn't been killed, she would have been arrested anyway. Hell, she might have even ended up on death row with all the collected evidence."

Jill asked about Yildiz. "She was released, and according to Intel, she's just disappeared."

"Disappeared? But..."

"They said they had let her go because of lack of evidence," Ian said.

"But I put in my statement that she had killed Leila, not that I give a shit about Leila."

"We don't get involved in local policing, Jill."

But when Jill mentioned Leila was an American, Ian gave her a half-cocked smile. "We do each country favors from time to time. This was one we did not care to dispute."

After her briefing and after being in contact with Kali, Jill received a call from Eric to discuss the immigration of Gabriella back into the US. "We've found Gabriella at CACU in Istanbul, and I've confirmed with her father that you will escort her back to the US. And Jill, there's more. Kali had received the manuscript from Matthew's biographer." Eric continued without waiting for a reaction from Jill. "I read it. All of it. He is one sick puppy, that's for sure. But I found two things interesting. Remember the two tt's the author spoke about? It turns out, according to the manuscript, that Matthew was referring to a double cross."

"Double cross. But... how?"

"The other thing is that you share something in common." Eric paused a moment, then continued. "He has your same gift, your RV gift. Albeit dripping with a mixture of psychosis and a dash of insanity."

"Mitch's bi-location," Jill sighed. "Mitch must have tapped into Matthew's energy field or something."

"Well, I'm not sure I'd go that far, Jill. But something is connecting the energy fields between you two."

"Are we landing?" Gabby interrupted Jill's internal review. Jill nodded.

When the seatbelt sign pinged off, they stood. "Let me help you with that," David said as he reached up and pulled out Jill's carry-on bag from the overhead bin, then lifted his finger knuckle under Jill's chin and gently kissed her.

The three of them walked through customs and into the arrivals area. A tall, dark-haired man approached, walking with a woman. The man stopped before them, bent down to Gabriella, and reached out his hand. "Hi Gabby, I'm Trace, your father."

ABOUT THE AUTHOR

This page is for authors to share their bio with their readers. How it is written will depend on the genre you write as well as your desired relationship with your audience.

The Author bio page is usually written in third person and shares information about the author such as where they are from, what their hobbies and sources of inspiration are, how and why they became an author, or why they write the type of content they write.

www.ingramcontent.com/pod-product-compliance
Lightning Source LLC
Chambersburg PA
CBHW071127170626
46809CB00002B/529